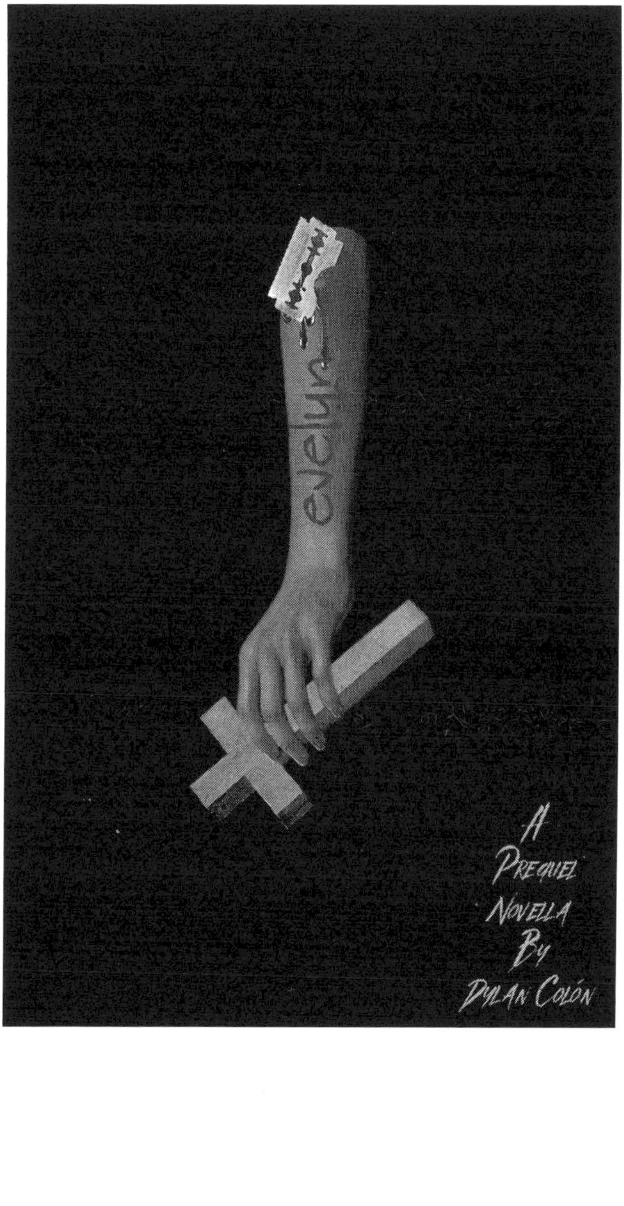
evelyn
A
Prequel
Novella
By
Dylan Colón

EVELYN

"EVELYN"
BY DYLAN COLÓN

EVELYN

CHAPTER LIST

Chapter 1
Emerald Crest Psychiatric

"Evelyn, how are you?"
"How am I? Are you serious?"
"Am I wrong to ask?"
"It's just a stupid question," Evelyn scoffed.

Mrs. Lisa Winters was assigned to be Evelyn's therapist at Emerald Crest Psychiatric. She was a beautiful and petite woman in her early 30's, with brown hair, and glasses. If she didn't reveal her occupation, one could easily assume her to be a librarian. She sat across a 21-year-old, Evelyn Singleton; the young adult also had a petite frame but was of average appearance. The only thing that stood out about her was she dyed her hair black. The traces of her natural blonde were tangled up with her shades of black; Evelyn, unlike Lisa, did look the part… she was a patient at Emerald Crest Psychiatric.

"Why is it a stupid question?" Lisa asked calmly.
"Come on; seriously, you're supposed to be smart. What kind of question is that? 'How am I?'"
"I think it's a decent question; it's the question I'd like everyone to ask me before asking me anything."

"But look at where we are. No, look at where I am. White walls, white clothes, white rooms, barbed wire fences, and surrounded by crazy people who are not feeling so good. Now again, what kind of stupid ass question is that?"

Before Lisa could answer, Evelyn out of frustration, pinched her arm and grunted. "Why did you pinch yourself, Evelyn?"

"Because I shouldn't curse. I'm dying to myself and I shouldn't curse anymore."

"I agree, but you don't have to punish yourself, Evelyn."

"Well good for you! The 'know it all' therapist knows what I should and shouldn't be doing! Am I supposed to take your word on everything because you write all of your words in a fancy notebook?"

"So I'm discredited because I keep a notebook?"

"You're disconnected at the very least."

"And if I didn't keep one, I'd be unprepared?"

"Huh?" responded Evelyn, who seemed to be overtaken by bewilderment.

"If I didn't ask how you were and instead, assumed how you felt, I would have just been one assuming things? I'd be telling you how you feel?"

"Speaking cryptically doesn't make you any more interesting or any less stupid," Evelyn said. She was obviously annoyed and repressing her rage. It was as if her body was a block of C-4 explosives, just waiting to detonate.

"No matter what I say, you're just going to flip my words and use them against me?" Lisa asked calmly.

Evelyn's face reflected rage, her eyes were building up with tears of frustration and embarrassment. The breathing grew louder on Evelyn's side of the room as Lisa remained calm and focused. "It's just a question, Evelyn."

"I don't want to talk to you," she responded quietly, while her hands were shaking.

"You don't have to talk to me, but you can't leave until the time is up."

"Then I'll just sit here and waste your time."

"Evelyn, you could never waste my time… I'm always learning."

Instead of a traditional response, Evelyn began to mumble what sounded like whispered nothings. Her words sounded jumbled and swift; whatever she was doing sounded repetitive. Lisa watched nervously while maintaining a mask of confidence on her face. She let Evelyn mumble a few seconds longer before quietly asking, "What are you doing, Evelyn?"

She stopped completely but failed to make eye contact with Lisa. Her head remained hung towards the marble floor with her long arms hanging loose on both sides of the chair. She slowly made eye contact and moved her messy hair away from her vision and said, "Praying for God to give me the strength to show you mercy."

The tension struck like lightning but Lisa couldn't allow herself to fall behind this mental chess match. She had to be quick and take a chance with her words when it came to this patient. Lisa laughed and said, "Girl, me too!"

After the silence… was a light chuckle from Evelyn, a reciprocated giggle from Lisa, and then they were both laughing with each other. It was the first peaceful moment of the session and hopefully a step in the right direction. Once the laughter started to gradually come to an end, Lisa followed up with hopes of riding the short-lived momentum. "See? I'm not all bad."

"I'm still angry," Evelyn remarked while trying to keep herself from smiling.

"I believe you, trust me. I know you're angry, and you probably have every right to be. But how could I know unless you tell me how you feel?"

"Since when does anybody give a sh-" There was an immediate halt and a deep breath. Both women gave each other a "that was a close one" type of look. Lisa smiled with approval as Evelyn rephrased her question. "Since when does anybody… care… about anything I feel?"

"Since right here, right now."

"I'll give you something."

"Anything. It can be disrespectful, happy, sad, random… just give me something that you feel."

"...I didn't like checking in," Evelyn said.

"Most people don't, but I'm interested in why you didn't like it."

"I felt violated… I felt dirty."

"Why do you think you felt those things?"

"Because no one is to look at me in that way. God has a husband set aside and his eyes are the only eyes that should be able to see me."

Evelyn was now transitioning into a third emotion; she was sad. Her anger turned into laughter, her laughter turned into sadness. Tears filled her eyes once more, but it wasn't out of frustration. She felt heartbroken and shameful.

"I'm sorry you feel that way," Lisa said. There was a gentleness in her tone and her words were wrapped comfortably in empathy. She found herself switching emotions as well, Evelyn wasn't a dreaded individual to her. Instead, she was looking on her patient with pity and desired nothing more than to ease Evelyn's complicated mind. "Hey… Evelyn," Lisa whispered empathetically.

"What," she replied irritably, with tears running down her face.

"You are not dirty. I want you to understand that."

"How am I not dirty? They saw me."

"Only because it's a part of the regulations"

"What?..."

"We don't want you to hurt yourself, Evelyn. They had to make sure you didn't bring anything that you could use to-"

"Kill myself!?" interrupted Evelyn; her scream was loud and aggressive. The door behind her immediately flew open, and in walked two larger male nurses. They dressed in white but it was nicer than the patient attire. One had a syringe in his hand, with a sharp needle sticking out.

"What the fuck is this!?" Evelyn defensively shouted.

"Guys! Everything is okay, don't do anything!" yelled Lisa, who was using her hands to signal the other two nurses to back off.

But before anyone could respond, Evelyn savagely launched herself towards Lisa and grabbed ahold of her shirt. It didn't take long for the larger nurses to subdue her. Lisa rose quickly from her chair and stepped out of the way. The sight of Evelyn screaming in terror, while swinging every limb she could, was a horrific moment to witness.

She had managed to get a few knocks in on both nurses before one stuck her with the needle. The squeaking of her shoes sliding against the marble floor was winding down by the second. As she fell asleep, it reminded Lisa of a baby that cries itself to sleep. She looked at the two nurses with a glare in her eyes. "I was okay, everything was under control until you guys barged in," she sneered.

They didn't say a word, they simply gave a nod and carried Evelyn's limp body out of her office. Once the door was shut, Lisa paced the room with her hands on her head. She walked towards the back window and stared out into the open scenery of Washington State's snowy mountains. Though it rarely snowed, it was like those beautiful white-tipped mountains followed you everywhere you drove.

She paid attention to the misty-gray sky and the well-kept lawn outside of the ward. If patients were feeling good enough, they had a wonderful place to go for walks and embrace good energy from outside these white walls. Lisa wouldn't break eye contact with God's beautiful designs until her nerves were calm and she could be strong enough mentally for the next patient.

Chapter 2
Unnecessary Burdens

Evelyn woke up slowly and waited for her sight to gradually return. The first thing she saw were the white walls, aged and stained. It wasn't the office of Lisa Winters, she was in a much tinier room. The front door was wide open and she could hear the many footsteps of other patients. Other men and women wearing white clothes, would pass by outside her door.

She was too out of it to take note of their pace and movement, but she could also see other nurses in white, who would walk past. The next thing she noticed was a brown teddy bear; it was cuddled under her right arm. Evelyn grunted, moved it out of the way, and sat up. Further to her right was another bed, with another female patient staring at her.

The other girl had the same smile as one who waited in anticipation, as you tried the food they cooked. The skinny-blonde patient just continued to smile with anticipation, Evelyn just stared back. "Teddy kept you safe while you slept," she said cheerfully. Evelyn gave her a skeptical look and used her left hand to grab the bear. When she held it out for the other girl to take, she frantically yelled at Evelyn. "Right hand, right hand!"

It was like giving someone a complicated math problem and pressuring for a quick answer. Evelyn held the bear dumbfounded and tired. The other girl snatched it with her right hand and held it close to her chest. "You can't do that!" she yelled fearfully.

"Can't do what?"

"You can't hold Teddy with your left hand!"

"What?"

"Ever! Never! Ever!

"Okay! Shit, I won't!" Evelyn shouted back.

The girl smiled as a crying child who gets its way but Evelyn immediately started to pinch her arms. The blonde patient was now the one staring skeptically as Evelyn pinched harder and painfully grunted. "Hey! Stop that! Now!" she yelled.

Evelyn obeyed and looked back at the girl. There was silence until she said to Evelyn, "You shouldn't do that with your left hand."

"I don't think I understand."

"Right is good and left is bad."

"Huh?"

"When I tap my foot, I only move my right leg."

"Whatever," Evelyn said, with her eyes rolled. She looked at the blonde girl and asked, "So what's your name?"

"Michelle," she cheerfully responded.

"What are you in for?"

"Hey! What's your name?" Evelyn paused irritably but answered, "Evelyn. So what are you in for?"

Wide-eyed, she whispered, "I have to find the files." Evelyn just stared at her with every possible look of judgment. It didn't phase Michelle, who was discreetly in search of "the files".

"I need to talk to someone, I don't belong here with you," Evelyn said, as she got to her feet. Michelle's eyes grew surprisingly wider as she frantically jumped up and said, "Wait! You can't leave!"

"And why not?..."

"You have to help me find the files!"

There was a playful innocence about Michelle. She belonged here for sure, but she wasn't the dangerous type. Michelle was very animated and spoke with both hands. But don't ever tell her that because she wouldn't know how to handle that truth. "Evelyn," said a familiar voice.

It was Lisa Winters; her presence had a way of radiating a calm sense of relief. Michelle looked pleased to see her and though Evelyn wouldn't admit it… she was happy as well. *Maybe Lisa will get me the hell out of this place.* "Evelyn, want to come with me for a moment?" Lisa asked.

There was slight hesitation but staying with Michelle any longer was never an option. She irritably made her way to the open door and looked at Lisa. "Want to walk with me for a second?" she asked Evelyn. Nothing was said, they just walked.

It wasn't that large of a building; it resembled an all-white hospital interior. There was a narrow hallway that stretched both left and right; they continued right. As they listened to the gentle taps of their shoes against the marble floor, there were a few nurses and patients around.

A young adult man was shivering and repetitively whispering to himself, as a larger male nurse led him back into his room. The narrow hallways appeared to have patient rooms to their left and right like a hospital. Some doors were closed while others, like hers, remained wide open. Lisa and Evelyn passed by a room where a woman, a young adult aged, was having a full-on conversation with herself.

"Ms. Crazy has more joyful conversations with herself than I've had with anyone, ever," Evelyn chuckled. Lisa reciprocated her rude but funny comment with a smile. "Evelyn… do you know why you're here?"

"I know this… I sure as hell don't belong here. This is complete and utter bull-" It was another victorious pause for Evelyn, who took a close call breath, before saying, "This isn't right, I don't agree with me being sent here. I'm not like these people." They were approaching the final door of the hallway, where a terrified voice of an elderly man could be heard from inside his room. "I'm not going to believe you anymore, you always lie to me! I don't have to listen to you! Just go! Go!" his voice echoed, with a rebuking tone.

Evelyn didn't dare make eye contact as she walked past the open room. Lisa would have felt uneasy herself, but these irrational one-man arguments have become a part of her regular day. The sound of their horrified voices made their self-talk all the more disturbing. In the dead of night, it wasn't uncommon to hear them crying, screaming, or even pounding their beds in agony. Sometimes medication helped the opposing voices inside their heads, but every patient was different. It could take a while for them to find an effective treatment.

The narrow hallway led smoothly into an open lobby. There were game tables, a television set, multiple chairs, open glass windows that put Washington State's beautiful scenery on display, and a sliding glass window. There were nurses behind it, who watched the patients and provided medication during the appointed time. "This is the hangout room," Lisa said cheerfully but calmly. "I don't know why you're telling me, I'm not staying here," Evelyn hissed.

"You never answered my question. Do you understand why you're here?" The walking stopped and they were now standing in the hangout room. "No crazy people at hangout today?" Evelyn sarcastically asked; she was clearly avoiding the question. "It's not time, hang out doesn't start for another hour," Lisa politely responded. She knew that Evelyn was avoiding her question, so she asked one more time. "Evelyn, do you know why you're here?"

"BECAUSE I TRIED TO FUCKING KILL MYSELF AGAIN! THERE! ARE YOU HAPPY?!" Before Lisa could respond to Evelyn's abrupt outburst, Evelyn started to slap her face repeatedly. "Hey!" Lisa yelled while stopping her self-inflicted blows with empathetic urgency. Evelyn quickly dug her head into Lisa's arms and wept as a teenage girl after her first breakup.

"Shhh, it's okay, you are okay," she whispered to Evelyn, who appeared hidden beneath her messy hair. The guilt and shame that she felt for saying a simple word was heartbreaking; *what unnecessary weight to carry.* It was all Lisa could think to herself as she held the newest patient of Emerald Crest Psychiatric.

Chapter 3
When I Met Lucifer

"Though it may or may not feel like it, Evelyn... I think we made a breakthrough. You finally said it, confessed it, and now it can be addressed," Lisa said from behind her desk. She held up an empty notepad for Evelyn to see, placed it on a stack of folders, and approached the seat that was planted directly across from her patient.

The "breakthrough" was nothing short of pure anguish to Evelyn; by the time it was over, some other patients made their way to the hangout room. These were men and women between the ages of young adult and walking copse. Everybody wore white; patients were made to match the color of what appeared to be a cross between hospital and institution.

A young mother to a baby doll could be seen nourishing it. An elderly man was mute and staring off into space. There was a young adult male by the name of Alex; if someone were to intentionally or unintentionally make eye contact, he would throw fits until calmed down by a nurse. Aside from that, he was extremely personable and charismatic. Alex resembled a skinny young adult with shoulder-length black hair. Some casual patients played cards and talked amongst each other by the TV. Patients at the tables had their own ticks and twitches to them.

The thought of mixing in with "these people" was infuriating to Evelyn. Jesus mixed in with the tax collectors and sinners of his age, but she understood all too well that she was no saint. This wasn't the same circumstances; Evelyn wasn't here to save the sick, she was sent here because everybody thinks she is "the sick". Jesus would tell her to get the log out of her own eye before trying to pluck a speck from a neighbor's.

In the present moment, Lisa and Evelyn were across from each other. The statement of making a breakthrough wasn't one that slips the mind, but it was the beginning of a terrifying truth. If she acknowledged what Lisa said, then she had to confront her encounter with "The Deceiver" once more. In lingering silence, Lisa was patient and content. "Silence doesn't always have to be deafening, it can be freeing. Maybe we can just enjoy it for this moment… I always try my best to find peace in the silence," she told Evelyn.

Evelyn agreed in thought, she wanted nothing more than to just "enjoy the silence". But her silence was always a dwelling place for the darkest parts of her mind. She tried her best to block out the memory of his reflection; his perfect existence had appeared behind her on a few occasions, in the mirror of the vanity she was only supposed to see her face in.

His hair was beautiful; it was shoulder-length and black. Perfectly placed on both sides, touching the tips of his shoulders. His frame was lean and cut. He had ice-blue eyes and his skin was tan. This beautiful man wore a white gown; it was comparable to something the angels would wear in Heaven. Lucifer is often depicted with intimidating features; sometimes he's a red demon with pointy horns, an arrow-shaped tail, and a pitchfork. *But when I met Lucifer... he was the most beautiful thing my eyes had seen in this world. And when he spoke to me... his voice was so calm and soothing, no word from his lips was without its elegant touch... even though his beautiful voice was the one who told me to kill myself.*

Chapter 4
A Voice In The Shadows

Cold sweat dripped from Evelyn's pores in the middle of the night. Considering the room's freezing temperature, this only served as evidence of her fear. The pearly-white appearance of Emerald Crest Psychiatric was now a nightmarish shadow. It covered every inch that the human eye could capture, and the little noises in the dead of night weren't any more comforting. Michelle was fast asleep with Teddy tucked comfortably under her right arm.

Evelyn turned over towards the wall and pulled the covers in closer. She couldn't fathom seeing something lurking in the shadows, so she shut her eyes. Terror-stricken by the potential of her own imagination, she shivered while hoping to fall asleep. The vulnerability she felt was unnerving; if something were to appear from the dark corner of the room, what could she do about it? Her body was covered but her ear was exposed to the cold air. Then the most haunting tone of voice spoke ever so clearly into it.

"Why do you keep telling yourself that you're alone?... when you know I'm right here?" The voice was like a man's emphasized whisper; a chilling tone with the most insidious intentions. There was an authoritative presence that came with the voice and it put Evelyn into a frozen state. "You won't look at me?... why is that?" the voice asked.

She was petrified; terror had stopped her dead in her tracks. Evelyn couldn't exhale a single breath without its repetitive shiver. She was reaching for something deep inside herself to answer whatever stood an inch from her body. "I'm a-a afraid... th-th-that... if I lo-lo-look at your face... I wo-wo-won't forget it," she fearfully whispered back.

The tension-filled silence was present before the voice hissed its sinister response. "You... are not wrong... many have seen my face and prayed in vain. They pray to forget me... but they never forget. I live forever... in the back of their minds, and I drive them all into madness... TO THEIR GRAVES."

"P-please," she cried with agonizing fear.

"I am unlike anything your eyes have seen... you can't fathom, you could never comprehend. My exterior is a mixture of colors you never knew existed... if you saw them, you would pray vainly to forget them."

"Pleaseeee," she quietly wept.

"The darkness isn't what they should fear. They should fear what they can see. I am shapes, designs, textures... you never could or would want to imagine... look at me."

"No," she fearfully cried to herself.

"Look at me!"

"I'm not going to," she cried louder.

"LOOK AT ME!"

"NO!" she screamed in anguish.

"Evelyn!" another voice shouted. It was the perfect interruption and it took a second for Evelyn to process who had shouted her name. It was Michelle. She stood overtop of Evelyn with Teddy still tucked under her right arm. "Get away from me!" Evelyn hissed.

"Evelyn, I-"

"Get away from me!"

"I just want to make sure you're okay! You woke me up with your crying!"

"GET AWAY FROM ME!"

Michelle crossed her arms, pouted like a toddler, and stomped back to her bed. While Evelyn wiped her tears and tried to control her breathing, Michelle got one last word out. "Don't wake me up again!" Evelyn didn't respond, she rolled her eyes and tried her best to fall asleep.

Chapter 5
Sinner

"Look... Michelle... I'm... sorry," said Evelyn, who was shamefaced. They were across from each other in the hangout room, eating breakfast. It was simple eggs and sausage links served with the choice of milk or orange juice. The patients who surrounded them looked half-awake and non-optimistic. Michelle continued to eat from her plate as Evelyn tried to find more words to say.

"Michelle... I... I am not good at this, this whole apology thing. I just... I don't understand myself sometimes... actually, I hardly understand myself at all. Who I'm going to be, how I'm going to feel... it's different every other day, you know?"

There wasn't a response, Michelle wasn't even eating her eggs, she was reading the ingredients list that was printed on her milk bottle. Evelyn looked around and saw Alex talking to nurses by the window, while they made sure to not make eye contact. Another patient was poking their eggs and sausage while staring off into space. "Don't talk to me like that, we've spoken about this way too many times," a female patient whispered to the TV.

So many little noises, silent ticking, and bickering amongst them. These tiny yet rapid moments in time served as background music for Evelyn. Michelle continued to read the words that were printed on her milk bottle. "Michelle, what are you reading?" Evelyn asked. The milk bottle was immediately placed back on the table and those innocent eyes were once again, looking right back into Evelyn's.

"Look, they are somewhere in this place; they are hidden in between the lines!" Michelle theatrically celebrated.

"Are you talking about the files?" Evelyn asked while trying her best to not sound as irritated as she was.

"Oh my stars, yes! Yes, yes, yes, yes, YES!"

"Okay… what can you tell me about them? Why do you need to find them? Michelle, I don't even know what they are."

"And nobody does…" she whispered mysteriously. Michelle's hands here waving as a witch's or wizard's would, if casting a spell. Her eyes grew twice their size, as did the excitement on her face. There was a female nurse who yelled, "Medicine!" from behind a sliding glass window. As soon as her words landed on the ears of the patients, they got up and began to form a line outside of the window.

"Do we have to take medicine?" Evelyn asked; hiding her true feelings with a fake tone was growing more impossible by the second. Michelle didn't answer, she got up and made her way towards the line. White walls, white marble floor, white gowns, white line; to leave her black lunch table would almost feel like giving in to "the system". Evelyn took a deep breath and followed Michelle.

Nobody asked what the pills were, they were quick to swallow them and return to their table. Evelyn couldn't help feeling nervous about what she was about to put in her body. Before she knew it, Michelle had already taken hers and it was Evelyn's turn to swallow the mystery pill. The nurse nonchalantly handed her a tiny cup with two pills and another cup with water. She looked the nurse in her eyes and downed them.

As Evelyn started to head back towards her table with Michelle, anxiety was tearing her insides apart. She pulled her chair out and paused for a moment. "You okay, Evelyn?" Michelle asked innocently. She looked back at her and responded, "Yeah, I'm okay. I have to use the bathroom though." Michelle pointed her in the right direction and she was immediately on her way.

The bathroom door flew open abruptly as Evelyn frantically rushed in. Nobody was there, so there was no awkwardness in running towards the toilet stall. She took a dive, pulled her hair back, and stuck her finger down her throat. There was immediate tension and throbbing as she gagged. Everything she consumed was rising aggressively to the surface but it wouldn't come out. Evelyn moved her finger in a circular motion and began to cough nauseously. Still… nothing.

She tried a third time and would choose to commit; her fingers were not leaving her mouth until everything spilled. This time she stuck three fingers down her throat as deep as she could. All three were wiggling in their ambitious attempt to call on the uncomfortable gag reflex. It answered… instead of pulling away, she pushed through it and moved her fingers faster and harder. Now she was coughing again, but she pushed through the resistance. Finally, it all spilled out as did her tears.

As she looked at the pile of liquid puke in the toilet, her mouth still continued to salivate. Chunks of her breakfast were floating around and there it was… the pill she had successfully ejected from her body! Evelyn sighed relief and wiped her mouth with the toilet paper that hung to her left. She couldn't wait to wash her hands; as soon as she approached the bathroom mirror, what she saw was pure horror. In thin razor-sharp fashion, the word "Sinner" was carved onto her forehead.

Evelyn shrieked at the gory sight of her flesh and quickly ran sink water over her open wounds. As the warm water drenched her face and her hands tried to wash the bleeding away, the water turned red and her face did too. The blood was now everywhere and she started to panic with eyes full of tears. The sound of paper towels being ripped from their home was explosive and full of urgency. She began to scrub the blood away with them but her skin was being torn off of her face in the process.

When she looked at her reflection, the words had been stretched into more open wounds and the blood was pouring from all parts of her face. She cried and screamed in horrific agony; unrecognizable was her new appearance. Evelyn dumped her bloodied face into the sink and drenched herself in more water. When she threw her head back up to look at her grotesque reflection, she was perfectly normal.

Both of her eyes grew wide with surprise as thin lines of tears streamed out of them. There was no more blood, no more letters, no more open wounds… she was perfectly fine.

Chapter 6
Why Are You Laughing?

Lisa Winters sat across a small group of patients in the hangout room. There were chairs lined up; they were indicating the obvious… group therapy was in session. Alex had the floor and was looking at the white marble surface as he spoke publicly. "I am like the most insecure-confident person you will ever meet," he stated.

There were giggles amongst the other patients but Alex took no offense, he laughed with them. "I know it sounds crazy but it's true," he laughed. Lisa smiled peacefully and asked him to explain further for them. Evelyn remained quiet and unresponsive to whatever this get-together was. She was encouraged by Lisa to join the group and deep down, Evelyn hoped that her participation would make her exit from the psychiatric ward go more smoothly.

Alex had everyone's undivided attention; the patients had their quirks but this was an articulate group. What was said mattered to everyone and this was something they had to look forward to every other day. Alex could feel the eyes on him but he wouldn't dare to gaze into them; he kept his eyes focused on the floor and further explained his statement.

"I am who I am and could care less what anyone has to say or think. But I feel like I'm ugly and that's why I hate having my picture taken. I don't even like looking at myself in the mirror. But at the same time, I am so confident about who I am. I feel like I'm smarter than everyone but I'm too unmotivated to try anything."

"Hold on a fucking minute," another male patient said defensively. The man looked irate in his eyes as he yelled at Alex, "You think you're smarter than me?" He had a New York accent that made him appear tough in the current moment. The man looked middle-aged with a few wrinkles on his face. Alex looked directly at the man and coldly replied, "Yeah, I do think I'm smarter than you."

The man looked at Alex directly and was quickly threatened to look away from his eyes. "What the fuck you gonna do if I look at you?" he yelled in retaliation. "Stop this, now!" Lisa commanded. The larger male nurses were approaching the commotion as Alex launched towards the man and punched him in the face.

He repeatedly landed high-volume punches on the man's face before being pulled off by the nurses. Everyone scattered like tiny fish in a pond, when the violence broke out; they were now standing off to the side in fearful shock. Evelyn found herself jumpy and this surprised her. She was normally the violent one in these kinds of altercations, but to see violence as a spectator was surprisingly scary.

Alex kept screaming about how nobody was allowed to look into his eyes and how it was all the man's fault. The other man was being held back as well; he was cursing up a storm and trying to get his own hits in. They stuck them both with the same tranquilizer that Evelyn was given and they started to grow limp at the same time. "Alex is so hot," Michelle whispered to Evelyn, who was not as romantically mesmerized by him. As far as Michelle was concerned, she was crazy to Evelyn.

Lisa looked exhausted and was struggling to recapture the mellow atmosphere of the group session. She shrugged her shoulders, laughed playfully, and said, "Anyone else want to give it a go today?" The room grew dreadfully silent as every patient looked away from her direction. Alex's outburst was indeed a hard act to follow.

But Evelyn wanted to speak, she wanted something to be on her heart. It was frustrating to feel like talking when the words had no existence. *Why do I want to say something? Anything. Maybe I want to help or serve some kind of purpose.* She put her head down and thought hard about what to say at a time like this. Michelle would be the one to break the silence at its most awkward moment, and her tone was all but inviting.

"So you think we're funny?" she asked Lisa challengingly. The leader of the group session seemed perplexed; she was caught off guard by this challenging tone. "No, Michelle… I don't think you guys are funny."

"You laughed after Alex was dragged into the isolation room, you're trying to make this a joke."

"This isn't a joke to me, Michelle," Lisa earnestly stated. It wasn't the response of a woman who took offense, but a response that came from a place of sincerity.

"Then why are you laughing?" The room was still silent and the tension was thick. Lisa had sadness in her eyes and a face with too many questions. She didn't know what to say at first, after the pause would come the truth. Her truth.

"Because I'm nervous, Michelle… I laugh when I'm nervous."

"And why are you nervous?..."

"I'm nervous because I want to help you… and I'm afraid of not being able to…"

"How can you help us, if you haven't been where we are?" asked Evelyn, who finally had her voice in the matter. Lisa's eyes were welling up with tears as she whispered, "But I have."

"You have?" Michelle asked; she was surprised by Lisa's answer and felt the immediate anticipation to hear more. Evelyn and the rest of the room had their eyes locked on the one who was supposed to be asking the hard questions. She looked back at them and gave the response they so eagerly craved.

"I know what rock bottom feels like; I remember it all too clearly… I used to depend on the medicine the doctors gave me; I couldn't even sleep without it… and I was Lisa Moore… before I was Lisa Winters."

She was powerful and still holding herself together. This was her truth and she was hopeful of it setting someone free. The eyes of lost treasures resembled the way hers used to appear in her reflection. They still gave their undivided attention as she continued to share her heart.

"You know, it was one thing to be broken by him physically… but to have my mind broken was a whole different cancer." The tears were no longer held back, they ran beautifully down her face as she told her story. "I mean it. I would rather him break my bones than break my mind again. Bones will heal at the given time… but the mind can feel like a lifetime of putting yourself back together."

Lisa wiped her tears, smiled like the strong woman she was, and said, "But in my lifetime, I found myself in a place just like this. Maybe not as long as some of you, but I HAVE been where you are. And it was hard, oh my gosh, it was hard," she passionately gasped. "But I made it through. And here I am, right in front of a bunch of beautiful treasures who remind me of myself. I do this because I made it out and I want to help every single one of you. So when you ask me, ‘Why am I nervous?'... it’s because I care enough to feel at all.”

There was a different kind of silence that followed. It was a hopeful one, a silence that comforted a group of touched souls. Evelyn just stared in awe of it all. Michelle smiled at Lisa and said, “It’s okay Lisa… I’m nervous too.”

Chapter 7
First Church Memory

In the toilet water, Evelyn saw her liquid vomit daily. It was oddly something she was growing accustomed to like the half-sided conversations she would have with Michelle. It was Evelyn trying her best to be loving towards her neighbor, but Michelle was obsessed with "the files". It was difficult to find some common ground when she had no idea what "the files" were. Every stray piece of paper or trash had to be analyzed by Michelle; "The Devil is in the details!" she would say. *Whatever, I give up. Do whatever it is that you do, Michelle!*

There wasn't much to do at Emerald Crest Psychiatric; Evelyn spent most of her time just observing the patients around her. *These people are all crazy... what does that say about me?* How could she not ask that about herself? The patients in their white gowns looked like lost sheep; they were just wandering about in their own little worlds. Evelyn knew that she didn't belong in their world and from the looks of it… maybe they didn't belong in her's either.

The entire atmosphere of the psychiatric ward was eerie to her. She kept forgetting that she had a relationship with Jesus that needed to be improved. But how could she possibly come to understand and find joy in the heavenly things, when life on Earth was already overwhelming? Nobody would understand her world and why she had this guilt-driven desire to pursue righteousness. The patients of Emerald Crest Psychiatric; they didn't have their minds set on the ways of her Lord, they had their minds set only on themselves.

But to see God in Heaven, one must die to themselves… at least that's what Evelyn thought. The desires of the flesh are deceiving, she learned this as a little girl. Evelyn recalls her earliest memory of attending church and it was with her parents. They were any other American family that believed in God, but not the regular churchgoers. The only reason they went was because the neighbors next door kept inviting them.

It was a Baptist church that was planted across the street from another Baptist church. There weren't many restaurants or stores in the area; the houses were far apart from each other. It looked like a normal southern community. The church towered over the grass, where children in their Sunday dress shirts were laughing and playing with each other. Parents, grandparents, police officers, church leaders, and very few young adults were what made up the congregation.

Evelyn recalls how unimpressed she was as a little girl; the inside of the building was so plain and stuck in its past time. The sanctuary was nothing special; wooden seats were wide across in size for large families, and the rows lined up from the back of the room to the altar. Murals of Jesus and the biblical depictions of some Old Testament stories were displayed on giant windows. At the time, Evelyn knew nothing of those paintings.

She felt anxious, uncomfortable, and impatient as she sat down with her mother and father. The service opened with the church choir singing over the most boring piano music. Their voices were novice and flat, their passion was traded for routine and repetition, and little Evelyn questioned herself about how long she could survive the boredom these older people appeared to be used to.

The music stopped and to Evelyn's surprise, the children were released into Sunday school. Normally, being separated from the parents she loved and trusted would be difficult, but the grown-up service was boring enough to make her optimistic about leaving. She would be with kids her age, in a room full of toys, with coloring books on the plastic tables, and kids' Bibles that included cartoon Bible characters.

As exciting as that may have been for a little girl like Evelyn, she only recalls one memory of her day in Sunday school. The older lady, who resembled a passionless kindergarten teacher, gathered everyone's attention and placed a hat on the table beside her. She gave the children a simple task… write some things you enjoy on a piece of paper and drop it in the hat.

She couldn't recall the name of the show or the cartoon characters she wrote on the paper, but that was exactly what she dropped into the mystery hat. The other kids lined up and one by one, they happily dropped their papers in the hat. Evelyn wasn't the only one excited and curious about how her paper was going to be used, all the kids were in childlike anticipation.

The lady smiled and said, "Okay, good. I'm going to draw paper from the hat and place them where they belong… do they go to Heaven or do they go to… the bad place? That depends on what you guys wrote. But don't worry about being embarrassed because nobody's names are going to be said out loud. This is between you and Jesus; if you wrote something he doesn't want you to like, pray for his forgiveness and that he lets you into Heaven."

Evelyn's anticipation and excitement were immediately contorted into fear. She was terrified of what she wrote being rejected and her having to burn in fire forever. Her mom always said she was going to go to Heaven when she died and that only bad people burn as punishment for their sins. But she was always reminded of how she was good and how God loved her. But now there was new information… she could be seen as bad and undeserving of Heaven if she wrote the wrong things on her paper.

The teacher was theatrical about the Heaven or Hell exercise, she would hold the paper up and sound so proud as she read off Heaven's entries. When something was bad, she theatrically pouted and said, "Uh oh, someone needs to talk to Jesus tonight. Heaven doesn't take kids who watch boxing with their parents." It was Heaven, Heaven, Heaven, bad place, bad place, bad place. With Evelyn's paper still not being called, her anxiety and fear only built up inside.

Then her worst fears came to life, the things she wrote were called out and thrown in the bad place pile. She was heartbroken and started to cry. The kids started to stare at her; some were curious and others whispered into ears about her not making it into Heaven. She couldn't stop crying, Evelyn had no idea that the shows and cartoons that she enjoyed were going to make her burn in that bad place forever.

The teacher tried to comfort her but she wasn't able to listen. Little Evelyn didn't want to spend the rest of her life in flames. She cried her innocent eyes out in the corner; her parents eventually came to pick her up. At first, her mother nourished her and kept asking what was wrong. Evelyn couldn't catch her breath, she kept sobbing and wiping thick tears off of her face. As soon as her parents could understand what happened, Evelyn's father picked her up and took her away. Fading into silence, was the sound of her mother yelling at the Sunday school teacher.

"We are so sorry this happened to you; never again! We won't ever take you to that God-awful church again! You are not going to burn in Hell for liking TV and cartoons! It doesn't work that way! Jesus loves you so much, honey," her mother passionately said in the car. Sniffles could be heard from the backseat and so could the angry comments that her parents made about the church. All the reassurance in the world couldn't erase the doubt of little Evelyn's salvation. She was so unsure of God's approval of her and terrified to suffer in fire. *My mom isn't a Sunday school teacher, what if she's wrong about Jesus loving me and letting me into Heaven? What if I'm bad?...*

Though this wasn't what Evelyn considered her "coming to Jesus moment", the fear of Hell was forever engraved into the back of her mind. She continued to watch her G-Rated cartoons and her regular TV shows that were made for a child audience. But she could no longer freely enjoy them. Of course, she was entertained for the most part; but at least once per episode, the thought of her screaming in fire would still cross her mind.

•••

Evelyn's skin had been burning on an endless loop, the fires were massive, and the flames raged on forever. Her voice remained at its highest pitch; it was painfully stretched and torn into shreds. She could hear the countless voices that surrounded her in this infinite fire… nobody ever stopped screaming.

She felt every bubble and sizzle of her flesh. If the pain and torment weren't so excruciating, she could begin to contemplate her sinful ways that damned her to this fiery pit. But she couldn't think about anything except the eternal suffering. The crackling flames were forever at the highest temperature, all the flesh that covered her body was forever boiling, God was forever gone, and she was forever nonexistent to him. This is her forever.

•••

"Hey, umm, are you okay?"

…

Evelyn was now awake, all of a sudden. She knew this wasn't her waking up from a deep sleep, but that she had lost some time in her day. She wasn't in the hangout room but standing in the middle of an all-white hallway.

There was a man in front of her; he looked around the same age as her. He was handsome; tall, skinny, and had thin blonde hair that hung perfectly around his glasses. The man wore the same white gown that all the patients had to wear. *He's beautiful.* Her fellow gown-wearing patient looked shy with kind-sensitive eyes; they were blue. He still had concern written all over his face but she didn't care. *God, just let him stand close to me, I want him to just exist a little bit longer*. Her trance was broken by his gentle and passive voice once more.

"What's wrong? I just saw you standing in the middle of the hallway. Do you need help? I can get someone." *His voice is so kind, so gentle.* Evelyn blinked a few times, as if half awake, she asked quietly, "Who are you?" The man peacefully placed his hand over the back of his head, innocently chuckled while blushing, and shyly answered her question like he didn't ask her one first.

"I'm John."

Chapter 8
Cemented

Evelyn didn't know what it was about John, but she was drawn deeply to him. There was a meek gentleness to his aura and she knew that he was safe. She couldn't help but wonder what a beautiful man like him was doing at a place like this.

"So… what's your name?" he asked. Evelyn continued to gaze into his ocean-blue eyes. *No way he's a patient like the rest of us, he's an angel of the Lord.* John chuckled nervously in a polite manner and scratched the back of his head. She snapped out of it and asked, "I'm sorry, what did you ask me?" He smiled beautifully.

"I asked what your name was. Take your time," he said playfully. Evelyn chuckled and told him her name. "See? Not so hard, right?" he asked sweetly. She just smiled and kept gazing into his eyes. Evelyn didn't realize how weird this may have looked to John, she was mesmerized by him.

"Look, I was on my way outside, it can be a little dead in this place… would you… like to join me?" he asked in sweet awkwardness. She didn't say anything back but nodded to his question with eyes that were spellbound.

They started to walk down the white halls, both of their feet were tapping against the marble floor.

Some patients could be heard talking to their walls from inside their rooms; nurses would pass them by and say nothing. John even greeted the lady who walked past them and received no acknowledgment. "Probably didn't hear me," he said, in gullible fashion.

Evelyn looked at him and smiled, but she didn't believe the nurse hadn't heard him. As they walked through the hangout room and towards the door, she thought more about the nurses. They weren't personable in the slightest. She didn't feel like they viewed her as on their level of humanity. The interactions were always quick and straight to business; for a place that's built to treat the human condition, it seemed like there wasn't much of an effort to engage the condition outside of medication.

They were outside and it was beautiful, the snowy mountains looked far more massive and God-like to her. Though the sky remained gray most days, fresh air felt better than air conditioning for the first time in a long time. "You know who I do like?" John asked excitingly, as they walked on the cement path that circled the outside yard. "Who do you like?" Evelyn asked quietly; she prayed her shyness wasn't mistaken for being rude or uninterested.

"I like Lisa Winters," he enthusiastically stated.

"Yeah… she's cool, I guess."

"You guess?" he asked with a peaceful chuckle.

"I'm sorry, I like her," she replied anxiously.

"It's okay if you don't, Evelyn."

"I like her," she more firmly stated.

They continued to walk along the path and allowed the sound of gentle winds flowing through the trees, to be their tension breaker. John looked ahead towards one of the benches and to his right, where he could see a patient picking tiny pieces of grass from the ground. His hands were in his pockets as he maintained that peaceful demeanor.

"I like Lisa because she isn't on a high horse," he said, bravely breaking the silence as he had been. Evelyn loved every moment of this slow-paced walk. The sound of birds chirping was better than the screaming and manic sounds of her fellow patients. "What do you mean?" she asked quietly, with her hands held against her lap and her shy eyes towards the cement path. He looked at her before saying anything, this was proving to be consistent. She secretly loved this about John.

"She has degrees on top of degrees, experience with people who hurt, and yet… I never feel like I'm being judged when she talks to me. Of course, she probably knows more than I do, but I've never felt her trying to show or tell me that. She's… she's-"

"Humble," Evelyn answered quietly.

"Yeah, she's humble," he replied with charm.

As the gentle tapping of their shoes hit the path, Evelyn was suddenly forced into a complete stop. John was bewildered and asked her what was wrong. She didn't know what to say, but her shoes felt stuck to the cement. "I'm stuck", she said with shock. He scratched his head and looked at the ground from where he stood. With his eyes on her shoes against the ground, Evelyn caught a horrific glimpse of her fingers.

Something tiny was wiggling from beneath the skin her nails were attached to. She thought her eyes had deceived her, so she looked closer with wide eyes. Tiny-white parasitic strings were slithering out of her fingernails. They looked like worms and were covered in her blood, as they were revealed to grow longer towards the ground.

She started to scream and cry with dreaded terror, as John frantically tried to figure out why she was panicking. Her thick tears and horror-stricken screams were of no help, as the parasitic blood worms slithered deep into the grass. She could feel her upper body being pulled off of the path and down towards the grass, but her shoes remained planted in place. She couldn't see or hear John anymore, *did they get him too?*

There were string-sized worms that slithered out from the tiny holes of her shoes, where the laces ran through; they dug through the cement while her body continued to be twisted and pulled towards the grass. Evelyn's screams were shredded as they pierced the air; her ankles were bleeding from being pulled down the cemented path, and her body was being torn slowly from being tugged towards the grass.

She could hear the bones in her back breaking; the human body was never supposed to move this way. Her skin was peeling off of her legs in chunks as she lowered into the concrete. In a few seconds, the opposing directions of her limbs were going to pull her apart. The last thing she could hear was her painful screams and the last thing she could see was her intestines slithering away from her body.

•••

The nurses ran as fast as they could and grabbed Evelyn. "Hey, hey, hey! You're okay! Stop, stop! Please stop screaming, you are okay. EVELYN!" yelled a familiar voice. It was Lisa; she was one of three other nurses, who circled above her. It was all coming into focus from where she was laying. The sky was still gray, John looked afraid for her, while he stood off to the side, and she still had her body intact. She took a deep gasp for air, looked at Lisa, and burst into tears again.

Evelyn
dylan colón

Chapter 9
Lost Ones

All over again, It was like Evelyn's first day at Emerald Crest Psychiatric. She sat across from Lisa in her office, but this time, less progress had been made. Evelyn had been sobbing for an hour, while Lisa remained quiet and supportive. Though there was a lot that Evelyn didn't understand, she was beginning to comprehend a comforting truth… Lisa could be trusted.

It was later in the night when Evelyn woke up and Lisa had stayed by her side as she rested. She was reading a book next to the hospital bed that Evelyn woke up from. Evelyn was now in a late night emergency session.

She didn't forget the things that John told her outside. Lisa wasn't on a high horse, if there was anyone she could open up to, it was her. Evelyn appreciated the silence because it meant that Lisa respected her; it would have annoyed Evelyn to be an emotional wreck while being drilled for behavior explanations.

Her sobbing had slowed down a great bit; breathing felt heavier to Evelyn as her exhales came out in choppy stutters. She looked at Lisa with shameful eyes full of tears, and said quietly, "I deserve this."

"Why do you think this, Evelyn?" Lisa asked gently.

"I ca-can't be good... I'm a bad person."

"I'm sorry you feel that way, I don't think you're a bad person." Lisa smiled with motherly affirmation, but Evelyn still hated herself.

"No… I am a bad person. That's why this is happening to me, that's why I see things."

"What do you see?"

Her sniffling was still present as the failed attempts to stop crying continued. Lisa was patient in waiting for Evelyn's words to reach the surface, she was hopeful about offering any form of comfort. She looked at Lisa; there was a mixture of pain, sorrow, fear, and guilt. "I see Lucifer… and whatever he wants to show me."

This wasn't the time to feel afraid or give any insinuation that Evelyn was crazy. Lisa maintained her gentile demeanor and approached this terrifying statement as someone who simply wanted to listen. "What does he say to you?"

"He tells me I don't belong to God… he says I belong to him." Evelyn couldn't hold the tears, they fell quickly as she held her face in shame.

"Why wouldn't you belong to God?"

"Because I can't be good!" she screamed ballistically at Lisa. There was another tearful breakdown from Evelyn after she shouted; Lisa remained calm and was determined to make her office a safe place for her patient. Evelyn had her head down with her hair tangled up. She started to slap herself in the face and Lisa wanted to grab her. But before she readied herself, Evelyn stopped the self-inflicted punishment and spoke quietly.

"Lisa… I'm sorry."

"It's okay," she answered sweetly.

"I can't belong to God because I can't be good. No matter how hard I try, I always get in the way of myself. Everybody hates me. My mother, my grandma, my father, my sister… they all hate me."

"I get it… and I probably get it more than you think I would," Lisa said affirmingly.

"You know what it's like to be hated?" Evelyn asked, with sorrow and desperation.

"By my family and by someone, I loved romantically. I was in a really bad marriage and because of that… I was always angry. My family rarely saw me during that time, but when they did… I took a lot of my anger out on them. I apologized, messed up, apologized, messed up again… I was eventually told, they didn't believe it when I said I was sorry."

Silence made its way into Lisa's office, as Evelyn wiped her tears. She took a deep breath and said to Lisa, "I want to tell you more, and I'm going to. I have to talk to somebody… but I want you to tell me more about how you were hated." There was no need to verbally agree, Lisa had already done that with her eyes. The only thing that Evelyn had to do was listen as Lisa always listened to her.

7 years earlier

The name "Lisa Moore" was printed on a mailed envelope that sat on the kitchen table. It was an electric bill. People normally stressed about these envelopes because of their financial situations, but Lisa found herself stressing for a different reason. She no longer wanted her last name to be "Moore".

She averted her eyes from the envelope and towards her belly, which had a slight bump. Lisa was three months, two weeks, and four days pregnant. The night was already here and she wanted more than anything to not be home. At any second, her husband would be back from work. There was always a 9 times out of 10 chance that he would be cracked out of his mind and angry. Crack cocaine was an all too familiar scent to her.

The man she used to sleep next to was now a nightmare that she couldn't wake up from. He used to be sweet and charming; the type to surprise her with flowers and an expensive box of chocolates. Her husband had a good-paying job and a promising future. Lisa used to love his way with words, his gift with them made her feel like the most beautiful woman he had ever laid eyes on. How could she not fall for him?

Lisa's family and friends couldn't be any more happier for her, they were just as hopeful about her finding true love as she was. Being in love has an energy of its own, everyone knows you're in a great place. The pure joy and excitement rub off on the people you love; there was a time when Lisa wondered if she talked about him too much.

It didn't matter to her loved ones, all they ever wanted was for her to be happy, and she was. Lisa felt lucky to be with him, she didn't want to mess this up. One of the hardest parts of falling in love is the fear of losing it. For her partner to wake up one day and decide that she was no longer enough for him... it would haunt her. But she couldn't control the future and he always reassured her that he wasn't going anywhere. They continued to go out on dates every week and get lost in each other's arms.

They fell fast and hard, eventually having a fairy tale of a wedding. It was everything Lisa ever dreamed of. The first few months of marriage were a dream come true, but after those first few months passed by... he stopped wanting to hang out with her family, and this meant she stayed behind with him. She would be asked to go shopping with her friends or to meet up with the girls at a restaurant, and he would pout like she was choosing them over him. She didn't want him to feel that way when he was the best thing that had ever happened to her. This is why Lisa accommodated him.

As the weeks passed by, he started to bicker about more things. If her mother called to talk to her, he complained that he wasn't being shown enough attention, then she had to hear his rant about how she never listens to him anymore. The same thing happened when she was invited by her friends to hang out. He didn't have any friends, and this was always held over her head when she wanted to do something apart from him.

What started as accommodating, became a fear of losing him. The fear of losing her husband would soon become the fear of him at all. He was too picky, too unimpressed, too clingy, too controlling, too much for Lisa to handle. Nothing happens overnight, people take a piece from you one day at a time. One morning you'll wake up and see that you're trapped. You'll ask yourself how you got here in the first place, and the answer will be... one day at a time.

Five years have passed and the abuse has gone far beyond verbal. Lisa gets slapped around for just about anything. Her dreams don't matter, her family is practically a distant memory, her friends have moved on without her, and the worst part about it was most people probably assumed she was just busy living "the married life". He had a good job, she needed him and he knew that. But lately, she imagined being homeless felt better than living with him.

Lisa dreaded the sound of the front door being unlocked, along with the heavy steps of her husband in his work boots. He was going to slur his words and reek of whiskey, crack, or both. Lisa used to hope her careful living would save her from his wrath, but now she knew better. There was no such thing as careful living, he was going to find something out of place. If her husband couldn't catch her in his excuse to lay hands on her, he was going to start something from nothing. Lisa lost count of how many slaps she received as a result of his own lies.

Sometimes it was more than slaps, Lisa had been punched in the face a couple of times. It started with her arms, legs, shoulders; anywhere but her face. Lisa still remembers her husband downplaying his abusive tendencies by saying, "It was only your arm, it's not like you got hit in the face." She tried to leave a handful of times, but her husband used to cry and apologize about his "moments of weakness". There was always this indecisive routine of putting her down because she "wasn't good enough for him" or begging her to stay because "he couldn't live without her." There hasn't been a routine in a while, now it's just always the worst of him.

He was livid when she told him they were pregnant, she hoped that having a baby would restore the love they had. Lisa also questioned if he ever loved her at all. When she told him, he screamed and tore the kitchen apart. She remembers him slapping her in the face and demanding she gets an abortion. She ignored him with hopes that he would think it over and warm up to the idea of the family they used to talk about. He said it was the baby or him, and she remained silent. When he stepped through the front door, she would know if his heart was warmed by their new blessing. It was safe to say that Lisa was the only one who felt blessed by having their child.

•••

Evelyn still had eyes full of tears, but they didn't shed on behalf of herself… they ran gently down her face for Lisa. "What happened when he came home that night?" she asked. Lisa hated this part of the story because no amount of healing could erase the way that night ended.

"He beat the baby out of me," Lisa whispered with grief. It didn't take Evelyn long to walk over to Lisa and hug her tightly. No words were exchanged, they cried together and grieved a lost one.

Chapter 10
Praises

Once the crying came to a peaceful stop, Evelyn was ready to leave. To be told things so personal by someone in a position of power was comforting. If anything were to break down the walls she had built for herself, it was Lisa being vulnerable enough to share her story. Only a humble person would do such a thing.

What was next? Evelyn imagined she would head back to her room, she didn't know the time but it couldn't have been too late. As they smiled at each other, Lisa felt moved by Evelyn's newfound respect for her. The goodbye was sweet and gentle, maybe Evelyn would look forward to her next session. This would be the moment she told her story to Lisa.

As Evelyn was reaching for the door handle, Lisa's voice was again present behind her. "Hey, Evelyn?..." The questioning tone wasn't disrespectful or challenging, Evelyn could sense nervousness.

"Yes?..."

"There's something I need you to do for me."

"Oh yeah?... and what could that be?"

Nervousness was written all over Lisa's face, whatever it was she wanted to ask of Evelyn, was something she felt uncomfortable asking. But there was a readjustment of posture and a deep breath that translated, "Here we go".

"I need you to start taking the medicine we give you. I know this isn't what you want to hear, but I really want what's best for you. I want you to make it out of this place and back to your life. I don't want you to see things anymore. If it doesn't work, we can try something else. I'm not giving up on you. If you don't follow the rules here, they'll never let you leave. And-"

"I'll do it," Evelyn said, to Lisa's surprise.

"Umm, wow!" Lisa said. Her eyes were wide as she held her chest. Evelyn still had a smile on her face; a smile of someone who felt at peace. Lisa had talked so quickly, so she was now conscious of speaking less frantically. Evelyn spoke her mind at Lisa’s request.

"I don't want to see things either and I don't want to be here forever. I get it. Like you said... if it doesn't work, we can try something else."

"You have no idea how surprised I am and how overwhelmingly proud of you I am as well!"

"Maybe, maybe not," Evelyn shrugged, while still smiling.

"Um, would you feel better if I was there when you took the medication?"

"I'd be a little more at ease."

"Okay, it's a done deal. Evelyn… I promise to watch every time they give you medicine. I'm not going to let anything happen to you."

"I know," Evelyn gently affirmed.

"Okay then! I'll... see you tomorrow," Lisa said happily with a wink. Before Evelyn opened the door, Lisa got one last sentence in. This time, it was useful information about her medicine. "It can take a bit to hit your system and start working, so just hang tight for things to get better. If you still see things, just remind yourself it's temporary." Evelyn smiled at her and this was all Lisa needed to see from her patient. The door was opened and closed; Evelyn had left and Lisa still couldn't believe how compliant she was.

The door closed behind Evelyn and she felt at peace for the first time in a while. But as soon as this sense of calm resonated, there was a thought that silently cast doubt. *How long will this peace last? Nothing you feel is ever permanent. You know yourself; it won't be long before you wake up on the wrong side of the bed. This has always happened. You can't be at peace because your mind would never allow you to be. Maybe for a week, maybe for a couple of weeks… but nothing ever changes.*

Evelyn was quick to remove the doubt from her thoughts and start walking down the white hallway. What would have normally been reflective marble floors, were now creepy dark hallways. What she needed was a positive thought to hold onto, something that was permanent, something that never goes away. At this point, she was clinging to any positive thought that she could. A black female patient crossed her path on the way to the lady's bathroom, and she saw that as her first opportunity for "positive thinking".

Lord, thank you for diversity. Thank you, Jesus, that no one is the same. Everyone is fearfully and wonderfully made. I look around this place and see a mixture of ethnicities, and-

You're only in this place because everybody hates you. How could your little sister ever see you as her own? That sweet girl won't even leave her room half the time because she's terrified of you.

Evelyn stopped outside of the hangout room; nobody was there and it would have been pitch-black, had it not been for the eerie street lights outside of the windows. The corners of the room were engulfed in shadows, demons could hide beyond her vision, further down the hallways. *Lord, get me to my bed safely.*

All she had to do was keep walking straight ahead, her room would appear around the halfway mark of the narrow path. She couldn't stand the silence and she didn't want to tune in to the whispers of the other patients in their rooms. Just walk straight.

As Evelyn took her first steps forward, she began to hear another voice, and the voice was faint. Because it came in the form of a familiar melody, she was indecisive over being fearful or hopeful. It was the voice of an elderly lady. "Ohh happy day… ohhh happy day," the voice sang wearily from the hallway to her right.

Just keep walking straight. Go to bed and stay away from that voice. That's what Evelyn told herself internally, before continuing to walk forward. "When Jesus washed… when Jeessuss washhedd," the broken tone sang. Evelyn came to a complete stop, at the intersection between walking straight or turning right. "He washed my sins away," it sang, as if heartbroken.

There was a deep breath that she normally took before doing something she knew she shouldn't do, and then she turned right. "Ohhh happy day… ohhh happy day." The voice grew louder with every step that Evelyn took in the darkness; fear was waging war against her curiosity at this very moment. "When Jeesusss washhhed… when Jesus washhhed." She was only a few steps away from where this heartbroken tone was singing its praises; there was an open door that led into a patient's room. There was only darkness from the inside, where this eerie voice sang. "He… washed… my… sins… a-way…"

Evelyn's heart was beating faster than she could ever recall, all she wanted to do was turn back. It was the praises of her Lord and Savior that led her to turn right. Before her desire to turn around became a reality, the lights inside of the patient's room lit up brightly. An elderly obese lady was naked in the middle of the floor; her legs were spread wide open as a public display. She was laughing maniacally and aggressively masturbating; all while singing the same praises that led Evelyn to her room. The tone was no longer quiet and heartbreaking, but aggressive and screaming wildly; it was finding it hilarious to mock her God.

All Evelyn could do was scream and flee towards the direction that she came. The singing turned into gravelly shouting and it was mixed with sinister laughter. She ran with no care of being caught or put in the isolation room that Alex was sent to. The tears flew off of her face, her shoes rapidly squeaked against the marble floor. Evelyn ran into what felt like a brick wall, but it was a male nurse that walked the halls on his night shift. He was black with no hair, muscular with broad shoulders, and was caught completely off guard.

"What are you doing?!" he shouted, as he tried to hold onto Evelyn. She was terrified, screaming and throwing the limbs of her body in all directions. The nurse grabbed her wrists and wrapped his large arms around her. With Evelyn's back to his chest, he yelled, "Calm the fuck down! I'm taking you to your room!"

"No! There's an old la-lady touching herself in the room back there!" Evelyn screamed desperately.

"There's no one back there!" he yelled; Evelyn was still squirming, trying to get out of his grasp.

"How can you not hear her?!"

"Hear who?!"

"The fucking naked lady down the hall!" It immediately occurred to Evelyn that she cursed, so her immediate reaction was to slam the back of her head against his face. The nurse let her go while yelping in pain; he received a deep cut above his left eye. Blood started to pour out of the cut and down his face. As he continued to hold his eye in agony, Evelyn started to repeatedly bang her head against the wall.

She had already cut her forehead open when the nurse collected himself and grabbed her again. "Stop doing this!" he yelled.

"I deserve to be punished!" she wept.

"You need to calm down!" he shouted, as he held onto her tightly.

"I'm sorry! I'm sorry! I'm sorry! I've sinned!" she cried. Evelyn was working herself to death and slowing down. It was like a child crying itself to sleep. The nurse didn't want to resort to injecting her because he hated doing that to patients. Other nurses were rushing down the halls and he noticed that some patients were now peeking out of their doors. He whispered to Evelyn, "If you can tell me where you saw the lady, I will check it out. But you have to calm down before they give you a shot."

Evelyn's body went limp immediately, but her tearful shivering still remained. "Oh-okay," she said with tears. The other nurses approached them with flashlights and told the spectators to go back to bed. Lisa was amongst them with worry written all over her face. "What's going on here?" Lisa asked. Evelyn's eyes were wide and fearful; her nerves were through the roof and causing her to shake. The nurse answered, "She just had a scare, I'm going to check it out."

He looked at Evelyn and with his eyes, he told her to lead the way. She gave an affirming nod and nervously walked down the hallway. Even with a pack of nurses behind her and them using flashlights, Evelyn found herself terrified of seeing the lady again. What she saw was evil, what she felt was demonic; that lady gazed into the depths of her soul while defiling herself under God's praises.

They were approaching the room and Evelyn felt terror-stricken by the thoughts in her head. She feared the lady's appearance, she feared the lady's demonic form making itself known, she feared the potential of a sadistic massacre on them all. But they were now right outside of the door. The nurse that appeared to have a soft spot or a sense of pity for her, gently put her behind him and walked into the room.

"Please be careful, sir!" Evelyn pleaded from the side. All they could see were the beams that shot out of his flashlight; they moved up, down, left, and right in a quick motion. Evelyn's heart felt like it was pounding out of her chest when he returned. The nurses looked at him with silence, but what they expected was an answer from him. The nurse looked at Lisa, the other nurses, and Evelyn… "There's nobody there, we haven't even occupied this room yet."

Evelyn started to cry helplessly and swear on everything that what she saw was real. They gently walked her back up the hallway while she kept crying. Though they were surprisingly comforting, Evelyn's manic confessions of the lady existing were going in one ear and out the other. "She was real. She was real. She was real," she kept crying pitifully.

They were finally outside of her own room when Lisa approached her gently. "Evelyn, we can talk about this tomorrow. Please hang in there. We're going to try our best to make these things go away. I want you to lay down, try not to wake up Michelle. Please, please, please get some rest and feel safe. Feel safe knowing there are people outside that door who are paid to watch over and protect you," Lisa whispered. Evelyn hugged her therapist tightly, gave a tearful nod, and stepped back into her room.

Michelle looked so peaceful in her deep sleep, Evelyn only wished tonight would be the same for her. She wiped her eyes, which were already burning from all her crying, and got into bed. The rest of the night was cold and silent. Her fears made it impossible to fall asleep, but her eyes remained shut.

I am going to lose my mind before I ever make it out of here. No... I am going to die or be possessed before I ever get help. I'm so tired, weary, broken, and burdened. Jesus... please give me rest and take this from me.

Chapter 11
Guilty Thoughts

John sat across the table from Evelyn in the hangout room; they were playing "War" with a deck of cards. The game was something simple to keep her occupied while not having to think too deeply into the rules. The deck was placed in the middle, bridging the gap between them. They would take turns drawing one card at a time and the one with the highest number won both cards. The player with the largest pile of cards when the deck ran out, was the winner.

Evelyn could care less who was winning *this stupid little game*, her mind was elsewhere. She couldn't close her eyes without seeing the naked lady. Her wrinkles and bruised skin, the way her entire body folded downward in multiple layers, she had no teeth, her thin-white hair was like that of an old witch from a "Snow White" movie. The lady's bald patches had revealed her decaying flesh and her odor was a rotten scent.

Her blasphemy towards her Lord was all she could hear; the manic tone that was accompanied by sadistic laughter was engraved into the back of her mind. Evelyn would lifelessly pull a card from the top of the deck and lay it on the table. John would smile and place it in the win or lose pile. If she hadn't been so traumatized, John's company would be appreciated.

She knew that John was worried about her, he was the first face that she saw this morning. Michelle was already eating breakfast when John charmingly asked her to join him. She was too dead inside to reject him. Evelyn hated the fact that her potential joy for this moment had been robbed by demons.

If there was something to be appreciated, it was that John was quiet. He was doing everything he could by just being present. He slid a card from the top of the deck, smiled, and put both of their cards in her pile. Evelyn, who was still like an empty vessel, did the same and won again. She didn't touch the cards, John smiled and moved them to her pile.

"H-h-hey, I-I-I… I thought th-th-that I told you already… we-we-we can't pa-pa-pa-pa play the television, Mr. Jones," a frantic patient said to a familiar nurse. Evelyn looked off to the side and saw that Mr. Jones was the same nurse that she ran into last night. From the outside, he didn't seem like a bad guy. Mr. Jones did all he could with her, given the circumstances.

"Hey, buddy, how about we play cards? You beat me last time and I really want my rematch," he said gently to the paranoid patient. "Th-th-th-they are listening to-to-to us through the speakers Mr. J-J… Jones," he fearfully responded. But it didn't discourage the kind nurse from putting the patient at ease, he whispered with a wink, "They could never hear us, I muted the speakers. We can hear the TV but no one can hear us."

"N-n-no way!" the patient rejoiced.

"Yes, way," Mr. Jones responded, as he gently led him to a table with playing cards ready to go.

Evelyn was moved by this, she looked back at John, who was patient as always. They locked eyes for a moment, but her eyes were filled with heavy burdens. The lack of sleep was beginning to show on her face. But John looked beautiful with his gentle charm and blonde hair; it was perfectly placed around his glasses.

She didn't realize her gradual increase in heart rate or the chills running through her tense body. Like a fiend, she could feel the sweat and a deep longing for his embrace. Maybe he would lay her on the table and push against her… push into her… skin to skin. Now the feeling of guilt and shame was hot on her trail; it chased closely behind her self-serving desires. But John interrupted her bittersweet temptation; he made a charismatic attempt to lift her spirits with a story.

"So, once upon a time, I had this therapist. I was new to high school, so I guess that gives some idea of how old I was. Anyways, my mom begs and begs and begs me to see this guy, because I'm super depressed. I eventually agreed, so next, I'm in the car with my mom, and I'm on the way to my first appointment. I'm nervous, irritated, I'm honestly just ready for this to be over." Evelyn continued to watch him enthusiastically tell his story, while she remained expressionless.

"Well, I'm called in and this guy is the most well-dressed dude I've ever seen. He had his legs crossed with a fancy laptop on his lap. I sit down and he immediately gets snappy. Dude starts saying he won't tolerate overdue balances, a lack of trying on my part, and all this other stuff. Then he's looking through my file and reading over the things that happened to me. He asked me if I drink or do drugs and I said I didn't. The guy acts all surprised and tells me he's shocked to hear this." Though Evelyn kept her eyes on John, her lack of facial expressions remained.

"So now, I'm pissed and feeling judged by the guy. I want to flip him the bird and tell my mother the session was over. He asked me another line of questions and was rushing me to answer them quickly. I remember having to think about how happy I was on a scale between 1 and 10; he's tapping his foot and repeating the question. My experience sucked! But the funny thing was when I'm back in the car with my mom and she asked me how it went, what I thought about him." Evelyn's lack of expression had slowly turned into unimpressed.

"The guy's name was Jerry and I remember cursing in my rant. I eventually called him 'Jerry The Bitchass Therapist' to my mom! She started laughing and so did I; we couldn't stop! Long story short, I went again and he was actually really cool. I went for a few months and never had the same problems. But the funniest part of the story is this… we called this guy 'Jerry The Bitchass Therapist' every time we mentioned him. After school, my mom would ask, 'So how is " Jerry The Bitchass Therapist?' and I would tell her his bitchass was doing just fine!"

John started to laugh to himself while looking at Evelyn; he hoped she would join him, but she didn't. She went from unimpressed to irritated and asked, "So that's it?" John's laughing started to go off rhythm as it slowed down. Once a few awkward chuckles transitioned into uncomfortable silence, all he could ask was, "What?"

"That's your epic story for the day? It's stupid, can I go now?" she asked, with hate in her voice. John looked confused and slightly crushed, where dignity was concerned. He was shyly stuttering his way to a whispered response before she abruptly got up. "I'm leaving, I don't have to ask you for shit," she hissed; some of the cards fell to the floor as she angrily left the table.

Chapter 12
The Fall

Evelyn's rapid footsteps were out of rhythm as she stormed down the white hallway. Other patients would wearily pass her by and she gave no second thought to them. All she wanted to do was crash land onto her bed and sleep… sleep the day away… sleep the week away… sleep until they told her she could go home.

She turned into the open room and crashed on her mattress. It felt like laying down was her desire until she naturally found herself curled up. Her arms were wrapped tightly around her legs, with her face pressed against both knees; she wept.

I have no home because they don't want me there. Everybody hates me and they have every right to. I'm sinful. I can't even look at John without having lustful thoughts. This is probably the most peace my mother and father have felt in a long time. I'm sure they argue less when I'm not there to ruin everyone's day. I bet my sister is finally comfortable enough to leave her room.

"Why do you run away from yourself, my child?" said the most soothing voice she had ever heard before. His voice was more than familiar, it was the only voice of an angel to inflict terror on her. She slowly looked up and there he was, in the corner by the door… Lucifer.

"Because through my eyes… he was naked," she tearfully whispered. His ice-blue eyes were beautifully empathetic and his olive skin illuminated in his white gown. The fallen angel was in his glory; he smiled as a loving father would smile at their child. He was of gentle spirit, as he stepped closer to her. When his hand rested calmly against her cheek, she whimpered in fear.

"Do not be afraid, my child… there is no shame when you are before me."

"Shame… is… all I feel," she responded with tears.

"And yet… had the fall of man never taken place… you wouldn't know he was naked through your eyes."

"The Lord warned them of the repercussions; they knew what would happen if they ate the forbidden fruit," she whispered defensively.

"That he did… but he never warned them of a serpent in the garden, he left out the part where someone else would speak to them. Why would he do that?" Evelyn was frozen with tears in her eyes and sweat on her face. Tangled black hair blocked her vision; she truly resembled a patient in a place like Emerald Crest Psychiatric. Evelyn had no answer. He gently ran his fingers through her hair and spoke once more.

"It was always my father's intention to release sin into the world. It was always his plan for you to sit shamefully before me." Evelyn rained silent in her whimpered state; Lucifer moved his black shoulder-length hair away from his eyes, and he continued to speak.

"You shouldn't have to feel this way for the things my father subjected you to. It's like creating a fish that longs for the ocean… but inflicting punishment when it fails to live on the land."

"You wanted to be like God and that's why he banished you from Heaven. You're the 'Father Of Lies', and you're against him... I won't believe a word you say," Evelyn whispered coldly.

"Am I wrong to have dreams of my own? Are me and the countless angels who followed, at fault for having our own desires?"

"You are," she tearfully replied.

"Then why create us with our own desires? He knew what this was when he started this. Everything was always about him. It was tiring. Do you know what it's like to want something for yourself while being constantly reminded of not being able to have it?" Evelyn remained silent, so he continued.

"You do know what it's like. I know how you long to be a mother-"

"Stop," she interrupted.

"But this illness he allowed you to carry has-"

"Stop!"

"Why would he give you such a desire, along with the constant reminder of how it can never happen for you? What kind of game is my father playing?"

"STOP!" she screamed with manic hatred. He looked on her face with pity and said, "My child, I am not your enemy… I am my father's enemy."

It was like the sound of a gunshot; Evelyn screamed and tugged her hair in agony. It was loud, high in pitch, and it was as if there was no end to it. She started to punch herself in the face repeatedly; all she wanted was for him to leave her sight. Her fist continued to smash against her nose until it finally exploded. Like a balloon filled with blood, her face was covered.

She didn't notice the nurses when they rushed in to save her from herself. There was a struggle to pin her down and blood was getting all over the place. Their white attire was stained with red and her mattress was too. She then felt a sharp sting go into her arm, so she jerked it away. There was a syringe poking out of her arm; it hung loosely by the needle. Evelyn's vision was getting blurry as she processed one final thought before she was out.

The next time I wake… I'll be strapped to a bed and trapped inside of Isolation.

Chapter 13
4 Through 20

"Isn't she just beautiful? Honey, this is your little sister, Valorie. Though Evelyn was only 4-years-old, she understood the importance of being a big sister. "Can I hold her, Mama?" she asked with her arms outstretched. Her mother looked at her father, and they both smiled at each other. Her mother was still lying in the hospital bed with her baby sister tucked comfortably in her arms. "Please! Mama, I want to hold my little sister!"

"You promise to be very careful?" her father asked.

"I pwooomise!"

Her father carefully picked up her little sister and slowly tucked her into her big sister's arms. Evelyn was sitting down, so she was able to use her lap as extra support. "Make sure to keep your sister's head up, Sweetheart," her father said gently. As Evelyn held Valorie in her arms, she couldn't help but feel an overwhelming sense of love in her heart.

"Always love and protect your little sister, Honey," said her mother.

"I will, Mama. And someday, when I get real good at being a big sister... I can be a mama just like you, and I'll have my own baby."

...

Evelyn was 8-years-old, and sitting across from her at the pink tea party table, was her little sister, Valorie. "Now Valorie, make sure to poke out your pinky when you take a sip," Evelyn instructed. Her little sister blushed and took an imaginary sip with her pinky in the air. "Did I do it, Evelyn?" she asked innocently. Her big sister smiled at her and shouted, "Good job! You did it!"

Valorie started to bounce joyfully in her chair as Evelyn poured imaginary tea into her cup. "Would you like some more?" she asked Valorie?

"Why yes I would," she responded with a wink.

...

"You might want to consider putting your daughter in honors classes," said Evelyn's teacher. Scarlett was amazed to have this conversation, her daughter was 9-years-old and performing at least three years ahead of her age. "I'm extremely proud of my daughter, she's an absolute joy around the house, an incredible big sister, and now she's performing so well in school. I'm just nervous that putting her in advanced classes will put stress on her."

"Oh, I highly doubt it. Your daughter is very intellectual, she can think and process the

information on levels far beyond her classmates. If there is anything to be nervous about, it's her growing bored and underperforming. She can be around other kids who can communicate at her level; Evelyn is very mature for her age," the teacher replied.

...

Joseph could hear Evelyn's TV from the living room. The sound of rapid gunfire was lingering in the background, he couldn't concentrate on the show he was watching on his own television set. He wasn't angry, he was actually happy to know that his daughters spent every moment they could with each other. As more sounds of gunfire blared from their TV speakers, he couldn't help but smile. "I raised some badass little girls," he said to himself, as he got up to ask them to turn the volume down.

The sounds grew louder as he approached their bedroom door. He could hear the playful laughter of his daughters. When he opened the door, they both lit up with joy and screamed, "Daddy!" Joseph didn't have a chance to respond; they hopped off the pink princess bed and embraced him. With his arms wrapped around his little girls, he took notice of what they were watching.

"Woah, now-now, aren't you a little too young for 'Rambo'?" he asked playfully.

"NOOO!" they both giggled.

"Evelyn, you are only 11, and your sister is even younger than you are," he laughed.

"SOOOOO," they responded in unison.

"Hey, I'm serious, girls! You need to watch something else," he said playfully.

"You can watch it with us!" Evelyn shouted joyfully. Her little sister followed with, "Yeah! Then we'll have a grown-up with us!"

"Well... that's definitely a good point," he said with a smile. His daughters started to leap for joy as he was pulled by both hands towards the bed. He was now sitting in between his most beautiful creations.

...

"She hit me, Mama!" Valorie cried. Her mother had to wash her hands to rid them of the food she was preparing. Once she dried them at the kitchen counter, her hands rested gently on Valerie's chin.

"Oh my gosh, Sweetheart! You have a black eye! EVELYNNNN!" her mother screamed. Valorie embraced her mother and cried into her shirt. Evelyn approached them as the angry 14-year-old; "What?" she huffed.

"Don't talk to me like that! Why is your sister's eye black?" her mother yelled.

"Because she was wearing my lipstick," she hissed back with eyes rolled.

"I don't care what she was doing! You don't ever hit your little sister! What in the hell is going on with you?"

"It's my lipstick, she shouldn't touch things that aren't hers," Evelyn scoffed.

"I just wanted to look as pretty as you!" Valorie cried.

"Well, that's impossible because you're too ugly to look like me!"

"EVELYN!" her mother shouted, before slapping her across the face.

...

It was later that same night, and Valorie was still heartbroken by her sister's actions. This didn't make any sense. Evelyn was always so loving towards her. There was a gentle knock on her door before it opened slowly. When she looked up, it was her big sister. Evelyn looked more heartbroken than she did. "I'm so sorry," her hero said tearfully. All Valorie could do was weep into her pillow; Evelyn cuddled next to her and held her all night.

...

A couple of weeks later, Evelyn felt amazing and euphoric, she didn't understand the reason, but she wasn't going to question it. Today was destined to be wonderful and she wanted everyone around her to feel it. She hopped out of bed, walked down the hall, and knocked on Valerie's door. "Come in," she yelled. Her little sister was just watching TV.

"Let's go to the beach!" Evelyn said enthusiastically.

"I'd love to go, but we don't have a car."

"We're going to make Mom and Dad drive us; we can go as a family," Evelyn said confidently.

That was exactly what happened, they went to the beach as a family. The day was spent with the warm sand running comfortably through their toes, the sun keeping them company, and the sound of seagulls over their heads. Valorie would jump on Evelyn's back and use her big sister as a float. She felt safe and knew her sister would never let her drown. Near the end of their day, the two sisters watched their parents from afar; they were eating ice cream while staring romantically at each other. It was a good day.

...

Evelyn had been on this euphoric positivity for a couple of months. But she oddly felt the opposite today. In her mind, no one matched her intelligence and this made her irritable. Valorie used more milk than cereal that morning; "Stop being stupid, you don't pour that much in," Evelyn snapped, as she grabbed the bowl and drained most of the milk. She irritably slid the bowl back to her sister, who had a confused look on her face.

Later that day, her mother wanted to get a few groceries for dinner and they got into an argument. Her mother wasn't thinking, she had better options for the ingredients but she insisted she knew how to cook. Her mother picked back at her about the attitude she was showing, but Evelyn didn't see herself in the wrong. Her mother needed to use her brain.

When they got home, her father wanted her to come to the living room for something and she told him to wait. For some reason, he was acting just as stupid as everyone else. He started to yell back about her 'moody tone and Evelyn denied any attitude in her voice.

A couple of weeks went by and she found herself at odds with everyone. Why didn't anyone want to use their brains lately? They just kept making stupid decisions. Her parents were sounding like broken records about this imaginary attitude problem they thought they got from her. She found herself being yelled at more. Valorie got on her nerves, especially. The worst was when her little sister brushed her teeth and left the cap off. She held the tube to Valorie's face and shouted about ruining the paste inside.

...

There were a few days of euphoric joy and Evelyn's family received the best of it. She took her little sister everywhere she went, was extremely helpful in the kitchen with her mother, and felt very affectionate towards her father. She hated golf but actually managed to enjoy it with her father. Life was on her side and nothing could bring her down.

...

Then a week of irritable emotions took Evelyn over completely. She was short, snappy, rolling her eyes, confrontational, and felt a sense of superiority over everyone. But it wasn't her fault that they couldn't think on her level. One of many things that annoyed her was how Valorie would tear up about everything. If she doesn't want to be called names, then don't leave the clothes in the dryer. If she doesn't want to get slapped in the arm, then she needs to watch where she's walking in the hallway. It was simple; don't bump into her and she won't get hit.

...

"I'm sorry to bring you here," said Evelyn's principal. She was now 16-years-old and constantly getting sent to the principal's office. Evelyn's mom wiped the tears from her eyes as her husband rubbed her back to comfort her. She was tired; these meetings used to be full of compliments, now her parenting seemed to be under constant judgment.

"What is it now?" Joseph said; he was just tired at this point. The principal looked concerned as he answered, "There was a younger girl who because of her religious beliefs, has to keep her face covered up. Evelyn pulled the covering off of her face, then went on a rant about the girl's God being an imposter." All Evelyn's mother could do was hang her head in shame.

"We really hoped that her going to church would make things easier," she wept.

"So your family is religious?" the principal asked. Evelyn's mother shook her head "No" and covered her face.

"An old friend invited her to church and she loved it. She's been so terrible to be around these past few years... there's always something. My wife and I fight

a lot more, our youngest daughter just hides away in her room all the time, and everybody is always on edge. We can't predict Evelyn's moods; she goes from good to bad, bad to great, great to a living nightmare. She's impossible to keep up with. She hates us until she's sorry, and this repeats over and over again. If I'm being completely honest... she's just overwhelmingly hurtful. That being said... our family doesn't do the church thing, but we hoped religion would make her peaceful. It did help for a month or less, but now she feels this obligation to hold everyone accountable for things... things that she feels are against God," Evelyn's father explained.

"Look... I don't mean to interrupt your train of thought, but this doesn't fix anything. I'm calling you both in because your daughter is getting expelled," the principal stated.

Evelyn's mother wept and shouted, "Expelled?!"

"Yes, this is just completely unacceptable. On top of this hateful act, your daughter has been an ongoing problem for this school. The teachers have had enough of her blatant disrespect and mood swings, and the students cannot keep dealing with her either. Your daughter is confrontational just to be confrontational. I really am sorry it's come to this and I hope she manages to finish her education... but it won't be at this school," the principal said sternly.

...

"Mom! Dad! I want to move back in! I hate being here by myself all the time!" Evelyn screamed. They were in the living room of her dirty apartment that they bought for her. She had religious decor on the walls, and they all hung crooked. Soda stains were all over the carpet, along with unfinished meals that collected fruit flies. Her parents stood their ground but they hated every second of this interaction.

"Sweetheart, you are 20-years-old, there is no reason for you to live with your parents any longer, you're a grown woman," her mother said carefully.

"Stop trying to make this about my independence! You only bought me this apartment so you wouldn't have to see me anymore!" Evelyn cried.

"You know that isn't true," her father said.

"Do NOT insult my intelligence! You're tired of me! You don't want to put up with me anymore! I'm here all by myself, so you can be your 'happy little family!',"Evelyn shouted in mockery; her eyes rolled and her voice was a cheap imitation of her mother's.

"That isn't true, sweetheart! We want you to grow up! We want you to be a functional adult in this world! What kind of parents would we be if we just let you live off of us forever?" her mother cried.

"This world?! This world?! This world is on the verge of judgment and we shouldn't get so attached

to it! I'm not trying to be like anyone in 'this world', I belong to God! I don't belong to the world!" Evelyn shouted with rage.

"What are we supposed to say to that?" her father asked hopelessly. Evelyn took a few intense breaths to calm down; she found her center and replied, "Don't say anything... just please let me come back." Evelyn's rage had turned into sadness. There was desperation in her tone and her body was shaking from nerves.

"I'm... sorry-" her mother was saying, but then she was interrupted by Evelyn's screaming. "Don't tell me you're sorry! Just let me come home! Please!"

"You're not coming home, Sweetheart!" her father shouted.

"I want to see my sister! Where is Valorie! I want to see my little sister!"

"You're little sister won't leave her room! That poor girl is terrified of you! TERRIFIED!" her mother screamed. To the parent's surprise, what came next was silence. It wasn't awkward and it wasn't tension-filled... but sad.

"Please... please take me back. I'll... I'll be better. I promise," Evelyn whispered tearfully. Her father took a deep breath and said, "You're not coming back, Sweetheart." All her mother could do was weep silently into her shirt. Evelyn stood still. She hung her head low like her mother's, her father held onto

whatever strength he could manage; he needed to stand his ground. "I'll lose my mind if I'm alone any longer," Evelyn whispered with sorrow.

Her father approached her slowly and gently kissed her forehead. "We're going to visit you all the time, we already do. It's time to be an adult," he whispered gently. Her father motioned to his wife that it was time to leave. Evelyn remained still and broken inside. Her mother blew the most heartbreaking kiss to her before they both left Evelyn alone. Something about the sound of her apartment door closing felt like the end of all hope.

•••

Evelyn woke up with an overwhelming feeling of pain and claustrophobia. Her nose was covered with a blood-stained bandage; she was laying in a white hospital bed, and it didn't take long for her to realize that she was in a different room. This room was much smaller than the room she shared with Michelle; this new room was meant to only occupy her. Everything was empty and white. Evelyn tried to move but felt restrained. She looked down and saw that her wrists and ankles were strapped tightly to the hospital bed. Her breathing soon turned into shivers, as she cried hopelessly in her new reality.

Chapter 14
If These Walls Could Talk

She had no idea of the time or how long she had been strapped to the bed, but she was tired. This wasn't the drowsy type of tired, but the weary and broken type of tired. Evelyn was burned out; there was no energy left to fight. She played around with the thought of deserving this.

"We all have a disease and that disease is sin." The voice came from the white walls that surrounded her; she was too drained for fear. But she recognized the voice, it was the voice of her pastor, Bryan. The distinctiveness and clearness of what was audible would have terrified her if she was new to this fight. But she remained limp and submissive to the restraints that bound her. This was why with tears in her eyes, she engaged with her pastor's voice within the walls.

"And here I am... left uncured…"

"I did my best to help you… my church did the best they could to help you."

"I know… and I'm sorry that I've let you down…"

"You let yourself down."

"You don't think I know that?..."

"Do you remember the sermons at my church?"

"I try my best but it's been difficult…"

"We preached the Gospel, we preached redemption through the blood of Christ."

"I remember…"

"You remember the first half of those sermons; you remember sin, the wrath of God, the punishment of sinful acts, the fires of Hell for the Godless and unrepentant."

"Those are hard things to forget…"

"But you don't remember God sending his only son to Earth, making him human like us, Jesus facing the same trials and temptations that we face, but living righteously and sinless, being without fault… then sacrificing himself on that cross to pay for your past, present, and future sins. You forgot the torture he subjected himself to because he loves you. Jesus took God's wrath in full, so you would never have to take it. You forgot that you are covered in his perfect blood, that it makes you righteous enough to stand before the holy God. You forgot that because of Jesus… it's safe to be all that you are… a human being."

"I don't know what's wrong with me," Evelyn wept. With the restraints, she couldn't wipe the tears from her eyes or the mess they made on her face.

Chapter 15
"I'm So Sorry This Happened To You"

The lights had grown much dimmer a while ago, Evelyn assumed this meant it was nighttime. The lack of a clock was making her time in Isolation drag on and it felt like she would have to live this way forever. The white walls continued to speak to her; they were clear and often disturbing.

She could hear them laughing at her; legions of demons giggled at her predicament. The voices spoke on top of each other and argued amongst themselves as to how she should take her own life. They reminded her of the sins she committed and that her family hated her.

But she was so tired; there wasn't enough energy for her to scream back at the many voices. Evelyn would try her best to fall asleep, but the demonic voices continued to keep her awake. They bragged about the eternal punishment she would endure in Hell and how Jesus didn't want to save her.

The door suddenly opened and there was a malevolent creature that stood before her. She wanted to scream for help, but she was paralyzed with fear. It was tall, lengthy, and had red skin with a harder exterior than that of human flesh. Its feet had sharp claws like that of a dragon's and they echoed throughout the room with every creeping step. Its nose was long and pointy, multiple horns were poking out of its head, and its facial features were indescribable. The most terrifying thing about this demon was how sharp its teeth were. Sharp claws wrapped around a briefcase it was holding. She was petrified as it smiled at her and revealed many rows of sharp teeth.

The sound of claws tapping against the floor moved closer to her bed. It never stopped staring and it never stopped smiling insidiously. The briefcase was placed on the ground as it reached inside. What the demon pulled out of the briefcase was nightmarish. It held a leather belt and attached to the middle, was a penis-shaped blade. Evelyn wanted so badly to scream, but she remained paralyzed with wide eyes. "Paimon sent me to check on you tonight," it said.

Evelyn's tearful stare had made its way back to this demon and what she saw was horrible. It had a lengthy erection and it smiled as it strapped the sex blade around its waist. Tears ran endlessly down her face as it reached a hand down the neck of her gown and pervertedly fondled her breasts. She continued to cry with terror as it moaned and felt her up. Evelyn gazed horrifically at the blade poking out where its penis was inserted and-

•••

She woke up to the feeling of her left breast being fondled. But when she looked up, it wasn't a demon that rubbed her nipple in the most uninviting way… it was a male nurse; someone she hadn't seen, who must have worked the night shift in Isolation. He was roughly grabbing her breast and masturbating over her body, which remained bound to the hospital bed. He moaned as he felt her up more aggressively.

Evelyn jerked her body to the side and let out a traumatizing scream. The nurse immediately pressed his palm around her mouth and whispered, "I suggest you shut the fuck up if you ever want to leave this place. And don't you even think about saying a word because nobody will ever believe a crazy bitch like you, over me. They'll keep you here forever if they think you're making shit up."

The nurse continued to pleasure himself to the sound of her cries and the feel of her breasts; his evil act was abruptly interrupted by a familiar voice that shouted at him. "What the fuck are you doing?!" Lisa screamed. She had Mr. Jones right beside her; he rushed the perverted nurse and pushed him to the ground. The evil man screamed in pain as he landed with his pants pulled down. Mr. Jones grabbed the piece of shit nurse and dragged him along the floor. There was a loud thud when the man's body was thrown against the wall. "Call the police!" he shouted, with his hands gripped tightly around the man's throat.

The sound of Evelyn's cries could be heard over the phone when Lisa called the cops. When Lisa freed Evelyn from her restraints, she was emotionally embraced by her beloved patient. "I'm so sorry this happened to you," Lisa whispered while holding Evelyn like a mother would hold her child.

Chapter 16
As Days Passed By

The nurse was arrested and fired; it turned out that an allegation had been made against him in the past. But the sad thing was what he told Evelyn was true… nobody would take the word of a "crazy person" over his. A handful of patients spoke about an incubus coming to visit them in Isolation, but going crazy was what sent people there in the first place. These were always written off as delusions.

Does every "crazy person" who sees and hears things, actually see and hear things? Or are they all just sick? Lisa was never afraid to ask that question. After all, Evelyn told her all about the dream involving an incubus and how she woke up to being molested. Evelyn's night terror and the act of molestation were happening at the same time. It was an awfully strange coincidence.

Lisa had a family emergency when Evelyn was taken to Isolation, but she booked it straight to work when she was informed of Evelyn's situation. The act of restraints and being held in Isolation was detrimental to her treatment; Evelyn was not the type of patient to benefit from that method. She understood if her patient continued to harm herself, there wasn't much she could do to keep her from that room. But if there was any chance in talking Evelyn into finding a better way to cope, Lisa wanted to take it.

She heard everything that disgusting pig said to Evelyn, one of those things was sadly true… if she didn't show progress, she wouldn't be able to leave. She imagined these last couple of days in her office, was a better atmosphere to Evelyn, than being alone in the white room. Lisa was pleased with Evelyn's willingness to open up about her timeline of sisterhood, the brokenness between her and her family, and the way she personally felt about those things. It broke Lisa's heart to know that Evelyn believed wholeheartedly, that she wasn't wanted by her family.

Did she hurt them time and time again? Yes. But could she have done any better? Lisa had no clue. This was a sickness that Evelyn never asked for and now it just got worse with her most recent trauma. There wasn't any push back from her normally feisty patient, Evelyn was too weary and drained to fight. Lisa stood by on watch, as her pills were swallowed and it wasn't like pulling teeth, getting Evelyn to talk about her life.

But this willingness to surrender to the rules was rooted in a weary spirit. Evelyn's presence appeared as one who was without a soul; she was completely dead inside. This was the last thing that Lisa wanted her patient to feel; she could only hope for progress once the medication kicked in. But this could very well be a long road ahead.

Rightfully so, Evelyn was traumatized by what took place, after she embraced Lisa, physical touch was hard for her. Evelyn would flinch at the slightest hand on her shoulder. She would talk to Lisa and burst into what looked like random crying sessions, but nothing was random. Evelyn went through something she never should have endured. The staff at this hospital are here to treat and protect their patients, not harm them.

It made Lisa sick to her stomach; people who had positions of leadership meant to protect but instead, they harm the very ones who need them the most. For a few years, she had known that disgrace for a nurse. He was always nice to her and they had good conversations, she thought he cared about the patients. But these kinds of tragedies happen every day; in foster homes, hospitals, churches, etc.

She hated seeing Evelyn more broken than before; she hated that it was because of something that happened at the place she worked. If there was anything to hate more than the act itself, it was when Lisa called Evelyn's mother. She expected the woman to rush her way to see her daughter, but that wasn't the case. She cried for Evelyn and so did her husband, but they kept passively avoiding any talks of coming to see their daughter. It broke Lisa's heart that Evelyn was right all along… she wasn't wanted at home.

As the days passed by, Evelyn remained submissive to the medication and her therapy. The sadness was lingering and her weary spirit never ceased. They had an agreement; whenever Evelyn saw or heard something, she would talk to Lisa or Mr. Jones. Those were the only people she trusted. There were still demons visiting her in the night and voices speaking through the walls. Though Evelyn would scream and cry, she was faithful in not harming herself. Lisa reassured her that the nurses would be there to help, and she informed them of Evelyn's condition. As the days passed by, Evelyn started to grow more familiar with other nurses who came to her rescue during an episode.

But all the familiarity in the world couldn't erase the trauma she lived through. It had been a little over a week and she hoped the medicine would eventually take away her delusions.

•••

Evelyn woke up screaming and saw Michelle and Alex above her bed. They both calmed her down and gave her comfort. She was surprised to come back from Isolation, just to see they had fallen for each other. Evelyn asked what happened and Alex simply smiled while saying, "She looked me in my eyes." Even off the heels of Evelyn's most traumatic event, this was enough to make her wide-eyed. "Congratulations," she told them.

"He didn't hit me and he didn't freak out!" Michelle joyfully shouted. It was the first time that Evelyn smiled since leaving that room. Michelle added with an excited whisper, "And he helped me find the files."

The files had actually been a torn page from the Bible. It had Romans 8:28, highlighted in yellow. "All things work together". Through all of the trauma, it was a blessing for people to understand Evelyn, and they each played a part in keeping her head above water. This wasn't the first time that Michelle and Alex were there to calm her down after waking from a night terror. Then there was John.

They sat together during all scheduled meals. She was far from talkative but he took it upon himself to fill in those empty spaces of dialogue. He would simply talk to her, and even though she rarely showed it… Evelyn loved to hear him talk. He told her why he was there, and the reason was very similar to hers. He was a devout Christian who wrestled with his sexuality. John had never acted on his lustful urges but the burden has always been heavy.

All he wanted to do was honor God with his life. But how was he going to do that with this type of struggle? He wanted to have a wife and kids someday, but he would have to be attracted to a woman first. The possibility of that seemed very slim to him and this took tolls on his mental health. To live day by day in the skin of someone you are not on the inside; what a burden to place on your shoulders.

He wrote a suicide letter to his family before taking a handful of pills. The letter spoke about his internal struggles and how he didn't want to live life so miserable. John didn't want to wait in anticipation, for him to fail at honoring God. He knew he wouldn't be able to honor him through his sexuality and that meant his dreams of a family could never happen. Why should he live if all that awaits is his failure?

But he didn't die that night, he was found and rushed to the emergency room. The next stop was Emerald Crest Psychiatric. So here he was, undergoing treatment for his incurable burden. Lisa made him feel better about himself; if God could offer any hope, it would be through her.

She was helping him come to terms with his sexuality and that he did truly love God. She reminded him that God understood him more than anyone and knew that John loved him. Evelyn was broken just like him and she was another who felt enough spiritual guilt to attempt suicide. They were connected by the thorn in their flesh. Sometimes Evelyn wondered if she was John's answered prayer. After all… if Michelle could find a soul mate in Alex, maybe John could find a soul mate in her.

Chapter 17
The Beginning Of The End

"You are so desperate to get rid of me, the meds may cause me to vanish, but don't live in denial… I am always there," Lucifer told Evelyn. He was sitting in the corner of her room. Everyone was in the hangout room, Evelyn wanted isolated prayer time on her bed. The medicine was working, she was seeing and hearing things less. The hope was to have a fighting chance at treatment.

"I rebuke you in the name of Jesus," she whispered.

"You're never going to be like other women. You'll never have children, you'll never be able to enjoy motherhood."

"In the name of Jesus Christ, I rebuke you."

"And poor John, his sexual preference would never allow him to have a child. Wow… you two may be meant for each other. You are both spiritually miserable."

"Leave, in the name of Christ."

"Women like yourself… they never find peace in this life. My father never loved you enough to give you peace. Instead, he's given you mental illness."

"Shut… up."

"I once gave you an out. I told you to end your life and follow me. But-"

"I REBUKE YOU! IN THE NAME OF JESUS CHRIST, I REBUKE YOU!"

•••

John was writing in his journal when Evelyn stormed into his room. Before he could greet her, she threw herself at him. Evelyn was kissing him aggressively and rubbing his penis through his gown. He didn't want to do this, but his body was reacting on its own.

There was no one around, his roommate was in the hangout room and no other nurses were present. Once he had a full erection, he whispered for her to wait a second. "Shhh, just let this happen. Please, let it happen," she whispered desperately.

She pushed him on his bed and climbed on top. John felt nervous and somewhat ashamed to go against his sexual preference. Everything was happening too fast, Evelyn already had her panties off and pulled his underwear off. Then he felt her warmth; he was inside her, while his body loved what his mind and heart resented.

Evelyn was riding him from on top; moaning and thrusting quickly. "Get off, I'm about to cum," he grunted, but she went faster and harder until he climaxed inside her. There was silence, she smiled and kissed his lips. As she climbed off, he asked, "What just happened?"

"You were cured, that's what happened," she said, before leaving his room.

•••

Evelyn didn't focus on the fact that John was avoiding her. She felt free without the voices and hallucinations. Days would go by and she would hang out with Michelle and Alex.

Whenever she ran into John, she was nice and tried to talk to him. She once whispered to him through the hallway, "Just let go and accept the change that God has for you." John would smile shyly, and keep walking. She felt good about herself, to cure his affliction.

As the days passed by, Evelyn just fell in love with the idea of routine. She ate when it was time, took her medicine when it was time, went to her scheduled therapy sessions, and even listened in on group therapy.

•••

"So, Evelyn… I called your parents and told them of your progress," Lisa said, from behind her desk.

"Oh yeah? What did they say?"

"That they were very happy to hear this."

"Even Valorie?"

"... nothing was said about your sister. But that doesn't mean she isn't happy to hear about your progress!"

"Yeah, I guess so," Evelyn said, with disappointment in her tone. After a moment of silence, Lisa enthusiastically said, "Evelyn, you are free to go home!"

"What?" Evelyn replied; she was surprised and holding her heart in disbelief.

"You are free to go back home," Lisa repeated with a smile.

"I can't believe it."

"Well, believe it. You've been consistently improving for a couple of months. The medication has worked and you keep getting better. There really isn't much else we can do for you. So… congratulations," Lisa said proudly.

•••

Evelyn was gathering her belongings when John said his goodbyes. He gave her his phone number and kissed her lips. "If you need anything… just call me, I'm here for you," he told her. She smiled, looked deeply into his eyes, kissed his lips, and said, "As you know, something terrible happened to me in this place… but I have no regrets or ill feelings towards our intimate moment."

As she packed her bags and left, John only wished he felt the same way. He wished Evelyn never threw herself at him, and moved at such a pace, his body responded faster than his heart and mind. Now he was alone in her room. Though he didn't share the same feelings, he was going to miss her company.

•••

1 Month Later

John was hanging out in his bedroom when he received the call from Evelyn. She wanted to see how he was; he told her he completed treatment, soon after she left. They talked about their lives outside of Emerald Crest Psychiatric.

Evelyn still wasn't getting along with anyone at home, but she hadn't seen anything or heard the voices while taking her medication. John had hoped to hear about a family being restored, but not all stories had happy endings. After telling her how great things had been for him, she broke the news to him… she was pregnant with his child.

•••

Many Years Later

I hate my life; sometimes I want God to kill me and end this bullshit. These were the thoughts John had about his new life. The day that Evelyn called him about their first child, was the day all joy was sucked out of his life. He didn't know it at the time, but he was right outside of misery's front door.

They got married very soon after she called. They didn't want to be unmarried Christians with a child. John did what he felt was right. He already found it difficult to live with the guilt of his faith coexisting with his homosexual desires; to have a child out of wedlock would be unbearable to them both. *Maybe this is God answering my prayer.* That's what he used to think to himself.

These days, he only enjoys his children. Especially David, his oldest son. Being a father was the only bit of good in his shitty little world. He was married to a woman, but still not attracted to the opposite sex. They had four children, three of them were a result of her pressuring and guilt-tripping him into their intimacy. Time had gone on to prove they had no chemistry.

He had grown to hate Evelyn deeply. She was unpredictable in her moods; when it was good, it was great. When it was bad, it was terrible. His wife wasn't always on her medication, but things were a bit easier when she took her pills. The problem was how they made her feel, or she would find consistent balance and mistakenly think she could go on without them.

Everything about him was wrong to her. *I can't even buy a 2 liter of Sprite, without her bitching at me.* John's entire being was living a life that he hated and pretending to be someone he wasn't. The kids adored him but his wife made all of their lives miserable. The only one to notice it was his oldest son. It was heartbreaking to know the others would grow up and understand how bad their mother was.

Over the years, Evelyn grew to be a fanatic over Christianity. Reading the Bible made her worse and she started to enforce strict religion on everyone. He hated her false narrative; she would tell people that she was raised as a Christian, fell away from Christ when she met him, and rededicated her life to God... after their first child was born. He had to be the sinner in her story.

Arguing with the crazy bitch, wasn't worth his energy. Years passed by, and she grew obsessed with her theological studies. Evelyn appeared to constantly change the way these scriptures were interpreted. Her religious rules would change very often, but John was just along for the ride. He had been pulled away from his family and friends because everyone was wicked to his wife. They moved to Virginia when he was offered a good job. Anytime he tried to answer the calls from back home, his wife never allowed him to hear the end of it.

Things eventually got to the point where her "good moments" meant nothing to him. *I hate this fucking bitch and so does our oldest son. I need to figure out a way to just take the kids and leave. But what would she do? This bitch scares me and she's capable of anything, I feel. What's pathetic?... the fact that I have to escape to this fucking garage, if I want any peace in my life.*

John could hear his wife's off-pitch singing in the distance. It made him sick to his stomach; she sang hymns and praises to a God she never obeyed. He wished he wasn't so meek, so non-confrontational, so afraid of everything. He would never win a shouting match with that woman, but it killed him to know he never tried. Instead, John was going to accept this was his life, as he watched his children grow up to potentially become these mini religious tyrants. As of now, they were innocent… but he hoped and prayed, they would never be like their mother. Sadly, he didn't want them to be like him either. *Lord, may my children be strong and grow to know themselves.*

•••

17 Years Later
(After Evelyn Leaves Emerald Crest)

Many patients have come and gone at Emerald Crest Psychiatric, Lisa remembered them all. Evelyn was always in the back of her mind and occasionally at the forefront. She wondered what Evelyn had made of herself after all these years. It would break her heart to find the illness had grown stronger and ruined her life.

This was why her morning at the grocery store served her well. She was pushing the cart down the frozen food section when she crossed paths with Evelyn's mother. "Lisa! Oh my Gosh, it's been so long! How are you?" she asked enthusiastically.

"I'm doing great, thank you. And yes, it really has been a while. Tell me, what's new with you?

"Ohh, nothing really, Lisa. Joseph and I just sit around and watch TV all day. We're not big on doing outdoor things. Indoor people at heart, we've always been."

"No harm in knowing what you like. How's Evelyn?" At the sound of her daughter's name, she froze like a deer in the headlights. The answer to her question wasn't going to be one she liked, this was what Lisa had feared all along. Evelyn's mother had failed to answer, she was still caught off guard by the question. But she forced a smile and answered Lisa,

"She's done quite well for herself. Though she's no longer married, she has four children and lives in Virginia."

"Oh my Gosh, that's wonderful! Boys? Girls? How old are they?"

"She has a 17-year-old son, a 12-year-old daughter, an 11-year-old son, and a 9-year-old daughter."

"I couldn't be happier for her, and if you don't mind me asking… who was she married to?"

"John, from Emerald Crest."

"Wow, I did not see that coming. It's a shame they didn't work out; John was a real sweetheart when I knew him."

"Well… according to Evelyn, he ran off. She told me he didn't want to be a father."

That doesn't sound like John. Lisa couldn't get that thought out of her head.

A Few Years Prior
(Oldest Son, David, Is 12-Years-Old)

Blood mixed with shower water circulated down the drain. If tears never shared the color of water, there would be three colors draining. Evelyn held her blood-covered hands, away from her face. She watched the last of her husband, John, wash away.

EVELYN
Continue Her Story With My
"This House Is Broken Novels"
AVAILABLE AT
• Amazon.com
• KindleUnlimited
AVAILABLE IN
• ebook
• Paperback
This House Is Broken
Part 1: A Religious Horror Novel
Part 2: An Anti-Religious Cult Sequel
Dylan Colón
A Religious Horror Novel
"Dark and frightening in the most realistic way"
"Great and emotionally impactful horror"
"One of the best horror/religion mashups I've read!"
Dylan Colón
This House Is Broken Part 2
"A fantastic sequel that will leave your head spinning!"
"A powerful story about religion, cults, and family"
"The horrors in this tale are firmly grounded in grim reality"

EVELYN

ACKNOWLEDGEMENTS

Thank you God, my mentors in faith, and everyone who helped shape my view of Jesus. I believe there's more grace and love than we could comprehend.

Thank you Lisa Valentine; for being a beta reader, making sure my writing was accurate to psychiatric wards and patients who wrestled with their mental illnesses. Thank you for sharing some of the most personal aspects of your life story and allowing me to craft Lisa Winters out of it! You're so brave and a wonderful friend to me!

Thank you to my mother(Teresa), brother(Michael), and Rainey Wood. Rainey and Michael, you both helped me with my creativity and crafting certain scenes. You kept it honest and prevented bad ideas! Rainey was also a beta reader along with fellow author, Byron Griffin!

Thank you to the bookstagram community and every reader of my work! Thank you to those who supported me at all times and thank you God, for the trauma that made my writing feel real to the world!

Thank you to everyone who wouldn't stop talking about Evelyn! You are the reason why this prequel exists! I did this for you!

-Dylan

EVELYN
Make Sure To Also Read
"Forbidden" By Lisa Valentine!
The Person Behind The
Character, Lisa Winters.
Available At Amazon
Forbidden
Lisa Valentine

MEET THE AUTHOR

Dylan Colón is not just an author of horror, but a passionate fan of the genre. His love for horror isn't limited to literature; Dylan considers it his favorite genre in film. He believes that God brought redemption to his crippling fear of irrational things and his learning disability that kept him from learning how to read and write during his early school years. Perhaps that is why he feels passionate about reading and writing; perhaps that is why he writes about the things that terrify him. Against all odds, he published his own books and will continue to do so! DareToDream and read if you dare.

MY LIFE STORY

"It's emotional, inspirational, motivational, and one man's story that I highly recommend"

"I wish I had this book a year ago"

"It took me until I was 40 years old to get to that place and 8 years later I have been inspired by Dylan's book, Trauma Takes A Loss, to find that again within myself"

"Trauma Takes a Loss By Dylan Colón • This is a very interesting read; so much so I'm not even sure how to classify it"

DYLAN COLÓN
TRAUMA
TAKES
A LOSS
MY STORY, MY TRAUMA, OUR HEALING

AVAILABLE AT AMAZON/KINDLEUNLIMITED/MY INSTAGRAM BIO

HELP ME OUT?

IF YOU'D LIKE TO BE A PART OF MY JOURNEY AND DREAM AS AN AUTHOR... PLEASE LEAVE AN HONEST REVIEW ON AMAZON! THE MORE REVIEWS I HAVE, THE MORE LIKELY MY NOVEL IS SEEN ON THE AMAZON MARKET! I WELCOME ALL THOUGHTS ABOUT MY WORK. BOTH GOOD AND BAD!

-DYLAN

DARETODREAM

(reviews on goodreads are awesome too!)

Made in the USA
Monee, IL
26 March 2022

2adda8ef-d190-4ad0-930a-cd1b1dadb465R01